Reaper

Kyra Leigh

A Paula Wiseman Book

SIMON & SCHUSTER BFYR

New York   London   Toronto   Sydney   New Delhi

SIMON & SCHUSTER BFYR

An imprint of Simon & Schuster Children's Publishing Division
1230 Avenue of the Americas, New York, New York 10020

For information about special discounts for bulk purchases, please contact Simon &
Schuster Special Sales at 1-866-506-1949 or business@simonandschuster.com.
The Simon & Schuster Speakers Bureau can bring authors to your live event.
For more information or to book an event, contact the Simon & Schuster Speakers
Bureau at 1-866-248-3049 or visit our website at www.simonspeakers.com.
Also available in a SIMON & SCHUSTER BFYR hardcover edition
Interior design by Tom Daly
Cover design by Laurent Linn
The text for this book was set in Arrus BT.
Manufactured in the United States of America
First SIMON & SCHUSTER BFYR paperback edition May 2018
2 4 6 8 10 9 7 5 3 1
The Library of Congress has cataloged the hardcover edition as follows:
Names: Leigh, Kyra, author.
Title: Reaper / Kyra Leigh.
Description: New York : Simon & Schuster/Paula Wiseman Books, 2017. |
Summary: "When Rosie dies in a car crash, she learns that before going to Paradise,
she must return to earth as a reaper and collect three souls"— Provided by publisher.
Identifiers: LCCN 2016048462| ISBN 9781481471961 (hardback) |
ISBN 9781481471978 (pbk) | ISBN 9781481471985 (eBook)
Subjects: | CYAC: Death—Fiction. | Future life—Fiction. | Soul—Fiction. | BISAC:
JUVENILE FICTION / Social Issues / Death & Dying. | JUVENILE FICTION /
Love & Romance. Classification: LCC PZ7.1.L4443 Re 2017 | DDC [Fic]—dc23
LC record available at https://lccn.loc.gov/2016048462

For Mom

Acknowledgments

I'd like to thank my editor, Paula Wiseman,
for giving my book a chance. She's truly amazing!

Thank you to Stephen Fraser for believing in this book, and for all his
kind and encouraging words. Also for being the Best Agent Ever.

To Laura, my best friend in the world—thank you for reading this book
numerous times, even when it was just a crappy first draft.

To Caitlynne—thank you for telling me you loved my writing,
even in the beginning when I wasn't sure I was even a writer.

And most especially, to Mom, for everything you've done for me.
Not only in the writing world but in the real world, too. Thank you.

1

After

"Miss Rosie Wolfe. Rosie Wolfe?"

I open my eyes. A girl shakes my shoulder. She wears a creamy-colored shirt with black pants. She looks to be about my age. Maybe a little bit younger. Her eyes look scared. Nervous, maybe.

"Thank goodness you're awake. I was worried you weren't gonna pass over." The girl hands me a piece of paper. *"She's* been waiting for you for ten minutes. She hates to wait, so you better get up and go to her office."

Then the girl leaves.

"Who?" I call after her. My voice comes out hoarse and tired. If she hears me it doesn't matter, because she doesn't come back.

That's when I realize I'm in a hospital. Only I've never seen a hospital room like this. The sheets are dark gray, and so are the walls. There's a cold feeling in this room. Like someone left the window open somewhere. I glance at the walls around me and there's not even one painting. When Dad stayed in the hospital, there were at least a few images of flowers and happy things. These walls are blank.

I get out of bed, walk to the door, and peek outside into a hall.

Two women head in my direction. They wear the same outfit as the girl. Flat cream-colored shirt and black pants. A few feet from them is a desk. Another woman sits there.

I take a deep breath and go to her.

She types fast on her computer, like maybe each hand is in a race with the other.

Before I can say anything, she speaks in a grumpy tone.

"What's the number say? Anne has yet to direct someone into the right room." She types for a minute more and then glances up at me. She looks like she hasn't slept in a hundred years.

"Uh, the nurse gave me this," I say, handing the old woman the piece of paper. She glances at it, and then back at me.

The air feels cold, but I don't have goose bumps. I don't even feel cold, but the air does. Like when I breathe, I can feel a chill on my lungs, or throat.

"It says, 'Go to room thirteen.' That means go to room thirteen. What's so confusing about that?" She holds the paper up for me to look at.

She has an annoyed look on her face. Like I've ruined her day.

"And if you believe that that girl is a nurse, then you're in trouble. If that girl was left in charge of someone's care, I can't imagine what would happen. Dead or alive," the lady says.

I feel my face go red. I shouldn't be embarrassed; I don't know her. Does she have to be mean? Is it part of her job?

"I'm sorry," I say. "I guess I didn't know which room that was.

Where am I? Is my mom here? Maybe staying in a different room?"

I can still hear Mom's voice in my head.

Calling my name.

Rosie.

She sounded so far away.

Just the thought makes me want to cry my eyes out in front of this grumpy old secretary. Or whatever her job duties are. Maybe she's the nurse and the last girl was the secretary? Either way, I do not like it here. If I wasn't sad before I certainly am now. This place is about as inviting as the hotel in a horror movie. Even the carpet is gray and depressing.

I hope Mom's okay. What would I do if something happened to her?

The lady laughs and shakes her head.

I didn't think it was possible to laugh without smiling, but I guess this lady has accomplished it.

"Just go down that hall." She points to her left.

I hesitate, and then walk down the way she points.

The walls are that same gross stormy-gray color. It reminds me of a dark cloud on a summer day. I hadn't noticed before, but some of the doors have numbers written on the front.

Ten. Eleven. Twelve.

Did my room have a number on it?

The farther down the hall I go, the bigger the numbers get. And the bigger the numbers get, the warmer the air feels. Everything around me seems to get brighter. I glance back at the nurse, and it's like a stormy sky hangs above her head. Even though she's just a little ways from me, she's almost in a different world. A sadder world.

When I get to the end, I see a big door with the number thirteen on the front. Next to it is a desk, with another woman in the same outfit as the first two. Only this lady doesn't look as grumpy. She's actually pretty. With light-colored hair, and bright skin.

For some reason when I look at her, I know something bad has happened.

Something awful.

As happy as she looks, is as scared as I feel. The more she smiles at me, the more I know fear. I probably look like I've seen a ghost. I feel like I've seen a ghost.

"Stay calm," I whisper, but it's hard to because I'm all alone with these strangers in this grim, depressing place.

Strangers and mean secretaries and nurses who have no idea where to direct people.

Just stay calm.

"Are you Rosie? She's been waiting more than fifteen minutes for you. What was the holdup?" When she speaks, her voice cracks, like she's spent her whole life smoking up a storm. I wasn't expecting her to sound like that.

I try to say something but she interrupts me again.

"Just go in. She doesn't like to wait." The lady gives me a funny face after she says this. My bad feeling gets worse.

I'm surprised when I walk into the room. There's another woman, yes, only this lady has long white hair, light skin, and glassy blue eyes. She wears a black dress and sits at a desk that I would imagine a rich businessman would have in his office.

"Rosie. Finally. Please come in. I don't have all day. Sit." The lady gestures to the chair in front of her desk.

This room doesn't look like it should even be in a hospital.

It's nothing like the halls or the place I just woke up in.

The walls have photos all over. Pictures of this woman with famous people. Dead famous people, actually. Gandhi. Elvis. Lou Reed.

Whoever did the Photoshop knows what they're doing. How did they make the images look so real?

I look back at the woman. She must be in charge here. She must be the one to help me figure out what is going on.

Am I sick?

Even worse, is Mom?

My hands shake.

The lady points to the chair again, so I sit. There's a stack of papers on her desk.

"Are you here to help me?"

Am I asleep? I hide my hands under her desk and pinch myself.

The lady glances at me.

"Are you a nightmare?" I pinch myself again. I can't feel a bit of pain. Maybe I am dreaming. I really, really hope I'm dreaming.

"Stop pinching yourself. Everyone thinks that the first day." Guess not.

I glance down at my hands under her desk. How did she know?

She sets a piece of paper in front of me. Tiny text covers the front and back, and there are two lines at the bottom that I assume are for signatures.

"What's this?" I ask. "And how did you know I was pinching myself?" She looks at me and smiles, just a little bit, but doesn't say anything.

A contract? It's hard to know because the font is so tiny. Whoever printed this didn't plan on someone reading it.

I start to panic, but I take a few deep breaths. Mom taught me when I'm nervous to just breathe, even if I have something to panic about.

Breathe.

Breathe.

Everything is fine.

This office smells like nothing I've ever smelled before.

It smells so good I can almost taste it.

Strawberries? Peaches? Why didn't the rest of this place smell nice? Out in the halls it almost felt sterile. Or maybe I imagined it that way?

"That's your work contract, and to be honest, there's no point in reading it. It's nonnegotiable. If you don't sign it, you're not free to move on." She opens a drawer and pulls out a pen. There's a black heart at the top. Like something I'd find in a party store.

"Sign at the bottom and I'll give you the first of the three names," she says.

She looks bored with me. Maybe she has somewhere else to be.

Either way, she's not very pleasant to be around.

Rude and impatient. And she hasn't even told me what's going on.

"Move on to where? Three names for what? I want to go home," I say. I glance down at the paper and then back up at all the pictures.

This woman with all these dead celebrities. All these look-alikes.

Am I in a circus or something?

"Where's Mom? Did she get hurt? Why am I here?" My voice starts to rise. I know I need to relax. Try to breathe, but I can't.

How did I get here?

Why is this happening?

"Who are you? What is this place?" I stand and back toward the door. Now my legs shake.

"Wait one moment," the woman says.

She gets out of her chair and walks to the door, then shouts, "Anne, I have had it with you. Your only job was to tell her and you forgot? Get out of here. You're on probation for the next seven days."

She slams the door shut and sits back down in her chair. She picks up the phone on her desk and clicks a number. "Hi, yes, that girl has been a pain in my ass since day one. I'd like her moved to a different department, please." She hangs up the phone.

For someone who just screamed her brains out, she's not even flushed. Her hair hasn't moved.

She's crazy.

I'm in a crazy home.

I'm in a peach-smelling crazy home.

My nerves must have gotten the better of me, and Mom must have admitted me.

Did I have a breakdown because of Dad?

"Rosie, I have some news," the lady says. She gives me one of those faces.

The faces that say, *I'm sorry but . . .*

"I knew it." Tears rush up on me.

I have lost my mind because of Dad.

The breathing didn't keep me sane.

Neither did the cooking.

I've turned into a total cuckoo bear.

"You didn't survive the accident," she says.

Accident?

She hands me a tissue.

Accident?

"Huh?" I say. I sound like a lost child.

"I know it's a lot to take in right now, but I'm busy. So if you could get the cry over with so you can start your work, I'd appreciate it," she says.

She doesn't look busy. She looks like she's trying to ruin my life. What accident?

"Is this some sort of joke? Who are you? Why am I here? This isn't funny!" I shout at the woman, and she doesn't even flinch.

Someone's playing a game with me.

Someone's trying to make me think I'm crazy. That's what this is.

"I'm not really crazy. I know this is a terrible trick," I say. I try to use a tough voice, but I sound even more like a crybaby than I did before.

"Carrie didn't like your outfit. You walked home to change. Only you never made it. Remember that white dog you tried to keep from getting hit by the truck? Do you remember now? You're dead, Rosie. It was your time." The woman uses a bitchy tone when she speaks.

But . . .

It all starts to come back.

The walk home.

The dog.

I saw that dog for three days. Then that evening it just appeared in the road. And that truck was going to hit it.

Mom calling my name.

The rain on my face.

"Good. You remember," the lady says. "I don't have the time or interest to let you grieve in my office. Take this information and get out. Thank you."

She opens another drawer and pulls out a folder.

"You'll get your second name after you gather the first soul. I'll be checking up on you. Me, or one of the girls."

I glance at the dead celebrities again.

This isn't where you go when you die.

None of this is right.

"If I'm dead, where's my father?" I ask. "My mom always told me when we passed on he would be waiting for us. That he would be here. We wouldn't be alone."

Mom and I talked about it a lot. It comforted me. Helped calm me down when I was missing Dad more than usual.

"I can't believe Anne didn't give you any of this information. Okay, here's the deal. You sign that piece of paper." She leans across the table and points to the line where my signature goes. "Then you take this name." She shakes the paper in front of my face. "And you collect the first person's soul. I send you two more. You collect *them*. And *bam*, you get to move on to paradise. Your dad will be there."

She pauses and lets out a big sigh.

"If you refuse, you get to stay here and work in the office forever. Or until something significant happens."

She sits back down and hands me the Sharpie.

"So what's it gonna be, Rosie? Because, to be honest, nothing significant ever happens."

I take the paper from her.

Someone's personal info is written on it.

Martin Gables.

I read about his job (retired garbage collector), his interests (walking his dog), stuff like that. There are suggestions, in bold, for how I might go about taking him.

Perching on his shoulder.

Pretending to be an injured animal.

Acting as if you have an important message to bring him.

I can't read anymore.

I think about that white dog again.

I fed him leftover food the night before I died. He'd come up on the back porch and scratched on the door.

I was nice to him. And then he kills me?

"I have to kill this person?" I ask. "I'm a ghost, and I have to kill people?"

Maybe I'm in shock.

I can't really be dead.

The woman puts her hand on her forehead, like maybe she's growing a headache in there. "You don't kill any of them. You bring them their fate. And you're not a ghost, Rosie. You're a Reaper," she says.

So that dog brought me my fate? It sounds to me like he killed me, caused my death.

"Haven't you ever heard of the Grim Reaper?"

I think of the cartoon Death with the hood and that long scythe thing. Even after Dad died, I figured, your body just stopped working, and you moved to your next life. I never thought some hooded figure came and took your soul.

"Yes, I've heard of him," I say.

"That's me. I'm the Grim Reaper. I bring death. And you get to help me," she says, holding out her arms. Like she's posing. Or modeling her tight black dress. I guess she does look nice in it.

It feels like I'm caught in a terrible fantasy novel. Something so unbelievable it can't be true.

This woman looks nothing like Death. She doesn't even look evil. She just looks bored, and annoyed. And classy. How can Death be classy?

"Why can't you do it? I don't want to do your job," I say. Who else will appear on this list? What if someone I know shows up?

What did this man ever to do me? This Martin Gables.

How can she expect me to take his soul? What if he has kids? What if he's happily married?

"Because that's not my job anymore. The only people I take are world icons. Like the pope, or Lady Gaga. See?" She points to the picture of her and Gandhi.

They both smile in the image.

I just stare at the picture.

She looks a little bit younger, but it's her all right. Gandhi looks exactly like he did in all the pictures I've seen of him at school, or on the Internet. Only this picture winks at me.

"What the hell? He winked," I say.

"There is no hell. Only work," Death says.

It's true.

I know in my gut, she's telling the truth.

"No more questions? Good. Now get out of here. Or stay and work with me forever. But the sooner you collect the souls, the sooner you get to see your father."

I stare at her for a second. Her face light, and her hair so fair. All of her so bright.

She's the reason Dad is dead.

I'm dead.

"Scoot!" she says.

I walk out of her office. Not sure where to go.

The door slams behind me. The lady at the desk outside of the Grim Reaper's office jumps.

"I'll get Brandy. She can walk you through the steps so you don't have to go back in there," the lady says. She gives me a face that says, *I'm sorry*. I saw that look on so many faces after Dad died.

The lady stands up and hands me a tissue.

"The shock will wear off, I promise."

She must know I'm dead.

Is she dead too?

The whole room feels dark and sad now. The bright feeling it had is gone. The sad gray walls. It's the type of place that would be cold all year round. The kind of place only the dead would be banished to. The kind of place you'd imagine your worst nightmare taking place. I breathe in deep and feel that cold air in my lungs. Even though I don't feel it on my skin, it's enough for me to get chills.

I suddenly want to cry. Just burst out into tears.

I want my mother.

My father.

I just want to go home. And from the sound of it, that's never going to happen again.

2

Before

"You can't wear that tonight, Rosie," Carrie said. "There are going to be hot guys. You know how long you've waited to actually meet a *hot* guy? Like, all summer long."

Carrie sat on her bed with a magazine. She glanced up at me every few moments to say what I was doing wrong with my hair, makeup, and clothes.

Even in her pajama shorts and tank top she looked pretty. Her long chocolate-colored hair was pulled into a side braid. I swear she's the only person who could pull off a side braid. She didn't even need makeup. Carrie was lucky to not have even a bit of acne on her face.

Unlike me.

"This is all I brought with me," I said, glancing down at my skirt.

It was a plain jean skirt, except a little shorter than my regular clothes. Mom used to hate when I wore it. But since Dad died a few months back, she hadn't complained about anything I wore. I think she was just glad I was getting out of the house.

"It's so . . . nineties. It reminds me of that guy who killed himself from that band. You know, the one my dad loves? That looks like something his girlfriend would wear."

Carrie tossed the magazine on the floor.

"Courtney Love?" I asked. My Dad listened to that old music too.

"All you need is a plaid vest," she said.

Carrie got up and walked to her closet. She pulled out a small black dress that was even shorter than my skirt.

"Try this," she said.

I held the dress up in the mirror. Just looking at it I knew it wouldn't fit.

I couldn't look at myself. The thought of putting something like this on made my face go red.

Since Dad passed away, I'd gained a few extra pounds.

"This won't fit me." I looked at my legs. At the cut on my knee from shaving this morning. Yet another thing to stress over.

"You could try," Carrie said.

She was trying to push my buttons, I thought. She'd been doing that a lot lately.

I didn't know if it was on purpose. But it sure felt like it.

Mom was worried that Carrie felt jealous of all the recent attention I'd been getting.

I guess Carrie wasn't used to sharing the spotlight.

And I didn't even want it. It wasn't even good attention.

Total pity party.

I hate pity.

"What do you suggest I wear?" I was annoyed, and I think Carrie could tell.

She shrugged. "Wear something black. It's slimming," she said, and then laughed like this was the funniest joke in the world.

All I ever wore was black. I brought the skirt because she told me I needed to add a splash of color to my life. I guess jean skirts weren't on her list of splashes.

"You're so hilarious," I said, grabbing my house keys from the dresser and walking toward the door.

"Where are you going?" she asked. She sounded bored with the conversation.

"To get something else to wear, since you don't like anything I brought," I said. All of a sudden I wanted to cry.

I felt so stupid. My beautiful best friend, with her perfect body, clothes, hair.

Me. Gross clothing. No father. Sad.

"I'm only kidding, Rosie. Wear whatever you want." She paused. "Except that." Carrie kicked the skirt I had brought.

"That's all I brought. So I'll pick something new, I guess."

"I'm sorry I hurt your feelings. Let's have a good night." Carrie hugged me, even though I didn't want her to.

My arms hung at the sides of my body.

I did not hug her back.

After the hug she sat back on her bed.

"Do you want to walk with me?" I asked. It'd been raining on and off that weekend. The gray skies kinda creeped me out. Even though it was just a couple blocks.

"Nah, I gotta get started on my makeup. Love you lots," she said.

She blew me a kiss and waved good-bye.

I was starting to hate my best friend. And I didn't even feel guilty about it.

3

Downstairs

"Did you sign the release forms?" A woman with dark skin and a curly 'Fro walks me around the building. Her name is Brandy and she's going to be my mentor for the rest of the day.

Show me the ropes.

Make me sign more paperwork.

All the stuff I didn't know you did after you died.

Did Dad come to a place like this? Did he have to go through this process? Sign papers? Hang out in the saddest place I've ever been?

"I don't know," I say, glancing into rooms as I pass.

Everyone in them looks asleep, dead, or sad. I thought life after death was supposed to be bliss. I didn't know it would be work. Whoever had the idea that working after a lifetime of school, work, and more work needs to be punished. I bet it was that woman. The Grim Reaper.

Before I met Brandy, they let me wash up in a bathroom. I almost didn't recognize myself. My skin is cleared up. And I'm not getting a stress headache, even though normally I would. The dark circles I usually have under my eyes have disappeared too.

"You can't go back until all of the forms are filled out. I'll have to double-check before you leave. We also need to figure out what you want to go back as." Brandy hustles down the hall.

"Back?" I ask.

She has a phone in one hand, and what looks to be a cup of coffee in the other.

Even in death people drink coffee. I bet Dad was happy about that. He loved coffee.

"What do you mean 'back'?" I ask. I follow her to another desk. She sits down and plugs her phone into her computer.

This all seems fake.

Like all of this is a set.

A fake.

Or a really stupid dream that I want to wake up from.

Even the desk we sit at feels fake. It's in a small cubicle. But something about it isn't normal. When I touch the walls, they are cold and hard, like glass. Same with the desk. I peek at myself in the reflection of the desk.

I still can't believe it's me staring back.

"Most girls go back as something angelic or light. Something not too noticeable. But you can go back as whatever, as long as it's not like a celebrity or something," she says.

"Back to earth?" I ask. I know it's a stupid question, but with everything she tells me, I'm even more confused.

Questions on top of questions on top of questions. Her

fingernails are gold and shiny. The color looks nice on her. Gold nails to go with her dark golden hair.

"We like to call it 'Downstairs,'" Brandy says, using air quotes.

"Can't I just go back as myself?" I feel light in my new skin. Almost beautiful. I never thought I could be beautiful.

But I also feel sad because Carrie will never get to see me like this.

No one will.

I'll never see any of my friends again.

Never hug Mom.

Never kiss a boy.

I'll see Dad, though. Maybe he's somewhere he can watch over me. Even though I'm already dead.

Does he even know? Does he realize I'm here? Does he know that I'm trying my hardest not to have a breakdown? He has to know. He has to know I'm here.

What about Mom?

"Oh, no. If someone recognizes you, we're in trouble. The living aren't fond of the walking dead," she says.

Then she laughs.

"Oh boy, we have had some horror stories. Someone slipped back as their own dead mother once. I bet you can imagine the drama that caused," Brandy says. For a dead girl, she seems pretty happy.

Happier than a lot of the people here. I wonder if that's why they have her walk the new people around. There is something calming about her.

"I don't want to change. I'm gonna go like this. No one will recognize me. I had really bad skin on earth. And I wasn't this small. Plus, my hair never looked this good," I say, running my fingers through my hair.

Did this girl know what I looked like before I died?

Would anyone recognize me?

Would Carrie?

"I guess you do look a bit different," Brandy says. She's taken a picture of me out of her top drawer and holds it up next to my face.

How did she get that?

"We'll still have to change the hair, but that takes all the fun out of it. My best friend, Lisa, she went back as a dove. It was a beautiful thing." Brandy smiles, like she's remembering Lisa fly down to earth as a dove. "I miss Lisa, but I'm glad she's in a better place."

Brandy sets the picture of me facedown on her desk and slides over to her computer. She types something into it.

"You're gonna have a lot more stress going back as yourself, just so you're aware," Brandy says as she types.

Dad was a fast typist like that. Unlike Mom, who only types with her pointer fingers.

Listening to those keys click away makes me feel sad again.

Dad would stay up late, typing new recipes for his latest cookbook. I stayed up with him sometimes. Especially toward the end, when he was getting sick.

"Can I call my dad?" I ask, looking down at my hands. They are so smooth. My skin has never felt so soft.

I don't know what the harm is in just hearing his voice. I haven't heard it in so long.

What about Mom? Where is she? I don't even bother asking if I can call her. She probably knows I'm gone. That I'm dead. I hope she believes that I'm in a better place. With Dad. Even if I'm not.

I feel a lump in my throat.

It's the tears. They have shown up to make things harder than they already are.

"Sorry, no," she says.

She glances at me and makes a frowny face.

It looks fake. I can tell she doesn't feel that bad for me, and why should she? I'm sure she deals with girls like me all the time.

Where are all the other dead girls?

In different cubicles?

I haven't seen one ghost.

Or Reaper, I guess I'm supposed to call them.

Us.

"I figured as much. Everyone around here seems to be angry and unhelpful," I say, then smile at her. "Sorry, I don't mean you. You've been the only nice person here."

Brandy smiles back, glances around, and then leans across her desk.

"I'll tell you what. If you don't tell anyone, I could make a call and check up on him."

Who knew flattery would work so well? Although it's true. She is the nicest person I've met since I've gotten here.

Has she met him? Did she help him when he died?

"Can you really?" I ask. I imagine that he's not in pain anymore. No cancer making him sick or depressed.

"Have you met him?" I ask.

"You can't talk to him, but I'll call Upstairs and see what I can find out. I'm kind of dating one of the higher-ups. Maybe he can help us," she says. "But no. I've not met any of the males who pass over."

Does everyone come looking for someone to call? Some long passed-on relative who was supposed to meet them at the Light?

"Thank you," I say.

I wonder if Dad's lying in the sun like he loved to do on earth.

"One thing for sure, Rosie. He isn't in pain anymore. No physical pain." She leans over and pinches me. Then she laughs and picks up the phone, and turns away so I can't see her. I hear her whispering.

Who is she talking to?

How in the world could she be dating someone up here? It's all so confusing.

But Brandy's right. There isn't any physical pain.

Except pain in my heart.

Mom.

For leaving her behind.

She must be so sad down there all alone. That thought makes me hurt on the inside.

Brandy turns around and hangs up the phone.

"You ready to get started?" She stands and straightens her top, then walks around the desk.

"Come on. Let's get you dressed. We don't have all day, and training takes at least an hour," she says.

She holds out her hand to me. I reach up and take it.

"This isn't as bad as it seems. I promise. It could be worse. You could have lived."

4

Back

"She wants to look like herself," Brandy says.

I sit in a salon chair. A young girl stands behind me and looks at me in the mirror. She introduces herself as Margaret. She has pink hair. It reminds me of cotton candy. And her skin is pure white. Like fresh snow.

Sitting in this salon I almost feel normal again. Like I'm out with Mom or Carrie, getting a normal haircut. Only they aren't here, and I feel nothing like myself.

This place looks like any other salon. Only the walls here are that same stormy color. But this room has a different feel. A warmer feel. Like I can breathe without stressing.

Before, I used to dread going to the salon.

All the mirrors.

People looking at my face up close.

Suggesting new styles to try out.

The last haircut I got was right before Dad died. The hair-stylist suggested I get a haircut that was long on one side and short on the other.

She had a similar style, and it looked great on her. But once she cut my hair short on the side, I regretted it.

When I got home from the salon and showed Carrie, she laughed in my face. I had to wear a beanie for a month.

"Yourself? You don't want to go back as some exotic animal?" Margaret touches my bangs when she talks, pulling me out of the memory of my awful haircut.

My hair looks so much healthier, I wonder why it wasn't like this before. At home it was so flat and boring.

"I would really just prefer to be human," I say. It doesn't make a lot of sense to me. Why would someone want to go as an animal?

Did an animal take Dad's soul, like one took mine?

Who could it have been? What could it have been?

"I wish I could go back. I would be a bird. I always wanted to fly," Brandy says. She sits on a chair a few feet from where I am. She looks at herself in the mirror. She takes a bottle of mascara out of her purse and applies it to her eyelashes.

"Why didn't you go as a bird?" I ask.

Margaret runs a comb through my hair. It feels nice being touched. Even though I've only been here a few hours, I already feel alone. And miss Mom more than I ever have. She used to brush my hair when I was in grade school. French braid it. Curl it. All kinds of things.

Then high school happened.

And Dad started selling his cookbooks. And Mom was baking

like crazy and didn't have time to help me with my hair, and I didn't want her to either.

"Oh, I didn't go back. I decided to stay here," Brandy says. When she says this she has a sad look in her eyes. She turns away from the mirror and glances at me. Like she's looking through me.

Like she's looking for something.

Someone.

A life before death.

"Why did you decide to stay?" I ask. I don't want to sound rude, but none of this makes sense. Does it make sense to her? Did it make sense to Dad?

Who would want to spend more than a few hours here? This is the kind of place where you get depressed and lonesome. I couldn't handle working here. Living here . . . or dying here.

"I didn't want to take the souls," she says. I imagine Brandy on earth, dressed as the Grim Reaper. Collecting souls and throwing them in a pink purse.

She doesn't seem like the type. But neither do I, yet here I am.

Will they make me dress like the Grim Reaper? Will they make me carry around a scythe? And when I walk down the street, will children point and scream at me with horror?

"Besides . . . in a few years they're going to reevaluate me, and if they think I've done a good job, they'll send me up. I won't have to collect any souls. Which I felt wasn't worth it. Plus, what are a few years when you're already dead?" Brandy says. Then she does a small laugh.

I don't really find any of this funny.

At least I have an option. Although I'm not sure if it's better than the one I was given.

"I guess I just don't understand," I say. The faster I get out of here the better.

"There are a lot of rules, Rosie. It's not as easy as just dying. There are loopholes to getting around reaping. It works for some of us, and others it doesn't," Brandy says.

Others, like me.

"You made the right choice, Brandy. I get my reevaluation in just six months. Cross your fingers for me, girls," Margaret says. Then she spins the chair around so she's looking at me.

"How long have you been waiting?" I ask. Is it like waiting for a raise at a job?

"Oh, they reevaluate me every five years or so. I think this time around I'll get to move on. I'm sick of working here," she says.

Brandy nods. "Same here."

Maybe they didn't make the right choice. It sounds like taking the souls is my only option. If I told Death no, would she make me come and work here? And fix people's hair, and have them sign all kinds of contracts?

"That sounds like a long time," I say.

Margaret waves her hand like she's trying to swat a fly. "It's worth it." Then she pauses and looks at me. "At least worth it for me."

It's like choosing between crappy and crappier. Both choices suck.

"Well? Could she pass as going back human?" Brandy gets up and stands behind me where Margaret is. They both look at me.

"We gotta change the hair, and probably have to change your skin color just a little bit. Are you going to be okay with that?"

Margaret's skin is so light. It reminds me of a porcelain doll I once had. Years ago.

She's the opposite of Brandy, who is all dark, except the way she talks. Light and airy.

"How long does it take? I want this over with. I want to see my Dad," I say. At this point I could go back as Big Bird if it sped the process up.

"Not as long as if you were to change species, so you're in luck. I heard that if you go back as an animal, you have to change back and forth between being human. So maybe this will be easier for you," Margaret says.

"Geez, can you imagine having to eat dinner as a bird one day, then changing back into a human the next, just to use the bathroom? Maybe I wouldn't want to go back as a bird after all," Brandy says. "There are just too many rules, too many guidelines."

I look over at Brandy. "You're really not selling this Reaper thing, Brandy," I say.

"Oh, stop. You'll be fine. Just take these so we can get started," Margaret says.

She hands me two dark blue pills. They both have Xs on them. "They'll knock you out. Once you wake up, you'll be good as new."

I look closely at the pills. What could the X mean? And what could a pill do to me now? I'm already dead.

Brandy hands me a glass of water. "Good luck," she says.

"I don't understand why I have to take the pills. I thought we didn't feel pain up here," I say.

Margaret shrugs.

"Because we can't have you moving around, Rosie. Just because you don't feel pain doesn't mean I want you watching me work my magic," Brandy says. She uses an annoyed tone, but then smiles at me.

"Just take the pills. It'll be over before you know it."

I look at the pills one last time, and then pop them into my mouth. I'm asleep before the water hits my tongue.

5

Pills

Before Dad died he had a lot of pills. It seemed like every type of pill sat in his medicine cabinet. Big ones, small ones, liquid gelcaps, herbs.

All of it.

He hated taking them.

Some days, when he seemed to feel real bad, Mom would grind up the pills and put them in a chocolate shake for Dad.

"I can't today," he said one morning. We all sat at the breakfast table, eating. Well, I was eating. Mom sat next to Dad and tried to convince him to take his morning medicine.

He looked bad that day. His skin almost gray. He'd lost so much weight. No one would ever think he cooked food for a living. Let alone ate family dinner every night. He was a shell of himself, and every day it felt like another piece of him broke off and disappeared.

"Josh, you must," Mom said. She stood next to Dad with a glass of juice and a handful of his pills.

Mom told me that I didn't need school those last few weeks. She said she knew the end was just around the corner.

I would have almost preferred to have been at school. Instead I was taking a vacation to watch my father die.

"I don't think I can continue like this, Shannon," Dad said to Mom.

I'd never heard him talk like that.

Sometimes he complained, but he never refused the medicine. When he said this, I felt a stab of pain in my heart.

That's when *I* knew this was the end. After today, everything was going to change. I don't know how I knew, but I did.

Dad looked defeated.

Sounded defeated.

"Fine. I'll blend them up," Mom said.

She walked into the kitchen and pulled out the blender and the chocolate milk. She threw in some ice cream and a little vanilla extract for flavor, and then flicked on the blender.

When she brought the shake back to the table, she looked almost as tired as Dad did. Only her eyes were so much sadder. Her eyes looked how I'd felt the past year and a half.

The hope was gone. Now we were just waiting.

"Drink that. It tastes great, added something special." She sat next to Dad and rubbed his back.

He shook his head.

It reminded me of a child who refused to eat his vegetables at dinner.

"I don't think I can," Dad said. He started to cry at the table. I walked over and put my arms around him.

Dad never cried. Not even when we found out about the

cancer. Not even when he stopped the chemo.

"Please, Dad. Please. Take the medicine. We hate seeing you hurt," I said. I tried to hold my tears in but they still slipped out.

"Josh, you can do it. Just pretend it's your favorite drink in the world. A drink that saves lives," Mom said. She didn't cry, though. She just rubbed Dad's back, and cheered him on.

"You can do it," I said.

Dad looked up at me and gave me a small smile. Then he picked up the shake and drank it all.

That was the last breakfast we had together. He died a few days later.

6

Still Dead

"Rosie, you're all done. Wake up."

I open my eyes to see Margaret and Brandy staring at me.

I feel weird.

Groggy, but in a way I've never felt before.

Almost like I'm floating.

So it wasn't a dream. I'm still here.

I'm still dead.

"You look so great," Margaret says. She holds a mirror and puts it in front of my face.

I have to blink a few times before my eyes can focus.

My skin is much lighter than I thought it would be. Great, now I really look dead. My freckles are completely gone, and my hair is black.

I still look like myself, but myself in a new body. The only things that haven't changed are my nose, eyes, and mouth. The rest of me is a different person.

"What do you think?" she asks, not waiting for me to sit up.

I've been moved into another one of the hospital-type rooms. Both Margaret and Brandy sit on the bed next to me.

This room isn't as gray as the others. It has light blue trim on the walls. It's a little bit more comforting than just gray walls. Even that little bit of a difference helps.

Brandy grabs a few pillows and props me up. I still feel groggy, and my skin feels hot.

Like I had a sunburn, but with no pain. Just the subtle feeling of heat.

"It looks . . . nice. Thank you. I'm glad you didn't change my eyes," I say.

People always said I had Dad's eyes, and even with this new face, I can kind of see him.

"I'm sure no one will recognize you without all those little angel kisses on your nose." She taps the tip of my nose.

She's talking about my freckles.

I nod. "I'm glad. I hated my freckles," I say.

Carrie used to tease me about them. Told me they were nerdy and childlike. Said that they reminded her of her mother's Raggedy Ann doll.

"Why would you hate them? It's rumored that the people with the most freckles were the most loved in a previous life," Brandy says. "I thought they looked great."

She sounds annoyed when she says this. Like it was my choice to erase them off my face.

It doesn't look like I was most loved in this life. Otherwise, I bet I'd still be alive. With Dad there too.

"Who cares. No one really knows," Margaret says.

She flips the mirror around and holds it up to her face. "I guess no one loved me in my life before."

Brandy laughs.

"Whatever." I sit up. The groggy feeling starts to wear off.

This is the second time today I've awoken in a hospital bed.

I don't like it.

"All right, we don't have much time left, let's get you up and ready to go," Brandy says. She gets off the bed and folds her arms across her chest. Then she looks at Margaret and smiles. "You did a great job!"

Margaret walks to Brandy and gives her a hug. "Until the next one!" she says.

"Good-bye, Rosie. Good luck. Hopefully, I will see you up there in a few months."

She waves and walks out the door.

"She was nice," I say to Brandy. I get out of the bed and put my slippers on. I can't get over how light I feel in this new body.

My body.

"I hope she has a happy afterlife," I say, looking at Brandy.

She lets out a big sigh. "That girl will never make it Upstairs. Not now, and not in a hundred years," she says. I follow her back out into the hall.

There are a few people walking around. They go in and come out of rooms. Maybe this isn't where people wake up after they die. This must be somewhere else, somewhere for the dead. Because there are a lot more people, and some of them are actually smiling.

"Why do you say that?" I jog up next to her. She walks faster than she did before. We must be on a deadline.

No pun intended.

"She just doesn't follow the rules the way she's supposed to. For instance, she never should have removed your freckles," Brandy says. She points to my nose. "Those are a big deal up here, and now that you don't have them, she's gonna get into trouble."

Would I get into trouble?

"Why? Why give her the option if she's gonna get into trouble?" I ask.

"Because it's all a test, Rosie. Everything you do."

Sounds like it.

A stupid one.

One I never agreed to, and I bet Margaret didn't either.

Tests. Rules. None of it seems fair. None of it seems right.

Brandy walks into another room. This time the room looks like a big closet of clothes. Most everything is white with dark bottoms.

"All right, Rosie, pick a couple outfits. Nothing too flashy, just something you think will go with your new personality," Brandy says. "We don't have many options. Since a lot of the Reapers go back as animals, they don't need clothes when they're out and about. Only when they're with their mentor."

I nod and walk around the room.

Some of the tops have words on them, but mostly they're plain. I grab three white tank tops and three V-necks, and then just black jeans and shorts.

"Not very exciting, but these will work," I say, holding one of the tops up to myself while I look in the mirror. The white doesn't make my skin look so pale, which I like. I've never dressed too flashy, so I don't really care what these clothes look like.

"Great, now let's get you off to class for training," Brandy says.

The training room is different from all the others. It's filled with girls, about my age. All of whom look confused and tired.

They all remind me of myself.

More dead girls.

More dead girls to bring more dead girls to bring more dead girls.

The place is set up classroom-style. There are small stacks of books on shelves attached to the walls. And a whiteboard at the front of the class. And next to the whiteboard stands a man holding a marker.

He's the first male I've seen since I got here.

"Rosie, you're late, which has made the whole class late," he says. Already I don't like this guy.

Brandy walks to the front and talks to him.

"It's not her fault, Charles. Margaret did a number on her," she says, pointing to my nose. Charles walks to me and puts his face close to mine.

He's pretty, with fair skin like me, and light-colored hair. He looks like he could be about twenty-five. Maybe younger.

"That she did. Well, someone's gonna get a bad mark for that. Whatever. Rosie, just sit down so we can get this over with," he says.

Great.

Another person with a bad attitude.

I realize that the dead are grumpier than the living. And I didn't think that was possible.

So much for finding happiness on the other side.

I choose a chair at the front of the class. All the ones in the back are taken. When I was alive, I preferred the front. But now I'm dying to sit in the back row. (Ha.)

I look around and notice something weird about all these girls.

Every last one of them has some sort of animal print tattooed on their hands. The girl next to me has a peacock feather. The one who sits behind me has a leopard print.

Before I can ask about the marks, the girl next to me leans in close and whispers, "What are you going as?" Then she points to my hand. I have nothing tattooed on me.

This must be what animals they are all leaving as.

"I'm going as a girl." I look down at my hands. "I'm going as myself."

Why does this embarrass me? Because I'm not going to be disguised as some exotic animal?

I just want to be myself. In life, and death, and then life after death. Maybe before I would have liked to have changed, but not anymore. Not now.

The girl looks me up and down. Then smiles and looks at the tattoo on her hand.

"I thought about doing that, but I've always loved peacocks. Good luck," she whispers. Then turns from me and looks straight ahead to where Charles speaks to us.

"All right, ladies, we need to get through this fast. The rules of life after death," Charles says. He takes the cap off the marker he holds and writes *The Rules of Life After Death* on the board at the front. Then he writes the numbers one through five below that.

Brandy lingers for a moment longer and stares at Charles, then leaves.

Could he be the man she loves?

"What do you girls think the first rule is?" Charles asks.

He paces the room while he speaks. I glance around the class. Only one person raises her hand. She has what looks like snake-skin tattooed on her.

"Don't tell anyone who we are?" she says, but she sounds unsure. Charles walks back to the front of the class with his marker. He doesn't respond to Snakeskin Girl. Instead, he writes next to the number one: *Befriend nothing, and no one.*

"Do you all understand what that means?" He points to the sentence again.

The whole class sorta nods, and says, "Yeah."

Charles looks at me, and then waves me up. "Rosie, come here real fast."

Why me? Why does he have to choose me?

I stand next to him.

My face feels hot, and my heart starts to race again. The panic. I need to breathe.

Relax.

"This is Rosie. She's the one who's making us run late. This little lady has decided to go back to earth as herself. Which means, she is at the most risk for breaking the first rule," Charles says. He taps the whiteboard where the first rule is. As if we all didn't read it, or hear *him* read it aloud.

"The consequences for breaking rules can be very dangerous. Not only for the living, but for the dead as well. If you hang around the living too long, your death can rub off onto them. Cause them or loved ones around them to fall ill. Sometimes even die," Charles says. He talks in a bossy tone, and I can't stand it.

He's worse than the nurses.

"How does anyone know if we break the rules? What if I

went back and made a friend?" Peacock Girl asks.

Charles shakes his head. "Not a good idea. No one knows for sure what kind of consequences until after it happens. But our friend Lady Death gets to decide that, and I highly recommend staying out from under her radar."

Why would anyone want to make friends on the other side? And why does he have to use me as his example?

Even in death I'm getting the type of attention I don't want. Just like when Dad died.

One girl in the back raises her hand.

"Yes?" Charles points to her.

"Why are you going as yourself? Don't you want to get it over with? Won't going as yourself complicate things?" she asks. The girl has a thick accent. Something I've never heard before. She has short black hair, and her arms are thin and brittle-looking. I can't see what's tattooed on her hand.

Charles looks at me, waiting for a response. I glance around the class again. Everyone stares at me like I'm some sort of alien.

Like I'm the only dead girl in the room.

"I don't know," I say quietly. Even if I do know, why do I have to share this with anyone? It's no one's business but my own.

"Oh, come on, Rosie. Just tell the class why you decided to go back as a human. Honestly, you're the first person I've had in class to go back as herself in a very long time. So I'm a bit curious myself," Charles says. This man doesn't stop talking, does he.

He can't just leave me alone. Leave me out of it.

I glance at the door, wishing that Brandy would come back and rescue me. But instead it's just another sad gray door in this sad gray place with all these sad, dead people.

"Because, I'm not ready to be someone else," I say. This

response doesn't seem to satisfy the class, or Charles, because he stands there and stares at me with a rude look on his pretty little face.

They really want to know? I guess I don't care what these people, no, these *Reapers* think of me.

"I'm not ready to be dead. And frankly, I'm not ready to do any of this. But I don't have a choice. So I chose to be me, and get this dumb job over with," I say. "It's not fair that any of us have to be here, you know?" I add, looking at Charles. The class nods in agreement. No one here looks like they're having fun.

"Why should any of us change?" I say. My tone is harsh and angry. "This whole thing is stupid," I say to Charles.

"Hey, hey! Settle down. Rosie, please sit back down. Thank you," Charles says.

"You're the one who brought me up here in the first place. Now you don't want me to tell you what I think? Well, I don't care, I think this is stupid. This is stupid and unfair," I shout, my heart racing. Charles looks nervous, like he's about to yell at me. But he doesn't.

"Sit down, Rosie," he says again. Only this time he uses a stern tone. Not the mocking one he was using earlier.

"It's true," someone in the back says.

Then the girl in the front row stands up. "She's right. I want to go back as myself. I don't want to be a peacock anymore."

"Relax, just relax, everyone. Forget anything Rosie said and pay attention to the rules. We don't have all day to listen to you ladies complain."

"But it's not fair," someone else says.

"Everyone, be quite now," Charles says.

The girl in the front sits down.

I walk back to my seat, with what feels like all their eyes on me. Having him point me out in class makes my blood boil. I didn't choose to be here.

Why me? A question I asked when Dad died, and now I ask again.

Do all the dead wonder it?

Do all those who lost a loved one ask it?

"Let's just get back to the rules," Charles says.

I fade out his voice.

I bet none of these girls deserved this. Or wanted it. No one wants to die. And to make things worse, I have to go back down there and make someone else die too.

Who gets to decide my fate? That woman upstairs? That Grim Reaper? Or is it someone else?

Who made this plan? I thought when I died, I'd know every-thing, and now I'm more confused than I was before.

All I know is this plan sucks.

7

Home

"**Sweetie, it's time** to get out of the house. Maybe you should go to the mall and see if you can get a summer job with one of your friends?" Mom stood in my doorway.

Dad had been dead for about a month.

The first week after his passing, Mom let me mope around the house. Sleep late, eat, or not eat. But after a while, she didn't allow it anymore.

I was sick of living like that, but I didn't feel like there was any other way for me to live.

"I'm too young for a job," I said into my pillow. I was lying on my bed, facedown. It felt like it was late, but it was hard to tell those days. "Plus, that sounds awful."

It all felt like a dark day. Like the sun hadn't fully come out. Like it was hiding behind the clouds because it was also sad that Dad was gone.

"Rosie, please. You're wasting your summer vacation. Get on out of bed and let's go for a walk," Mom said. She used that voice that made me feel guilty. I don't think that she did it on purpose, but it struck my heart in the worst places.

"I'd rather stay here. Let me know how it is out there, will you, Mom?" I used a sarcastic tone. Mom did a big sigh.

"Get up, Rosie."

I could tell by the way she said it that she wasn't playing, and also that she didn't want to be alone. And why should she be?

"Fiiine." I sat up and looked at Mom. She stood in my doorway. She looked tired, even though all the neighbors were coming by often and bringing us care packages and other nice things people do when a loved one dies.

"I'm glad to see that face. It feels like I haven't seen you in days," she said, smiling. She has the type of smile that could make the saddest person on earth want to cheer up. At least for a second.

I got up and opened my closet door. All my clothes sat in a pile on the floor. I hadn't done laundry in weeks.

Mom walked in and grabbed one of the few shirts that hung in my closet.

"Why don't you wear this?" she asked.

The shirt was pink with tiny flowers on it. Something my grandma bought me years before. It still had the JCPenney tags on it.

It was so ugly. Why did I bother to keep it?

"You've never worn it, Rosie," she said, looking at the price. Grandma didn't spend much on it. She was cheap.

"But it's so ugly." I grabbed the shirt from Mom and held it out to myself. "Plus, it will never fit me now. I'd look terrible."

"Rosie! I don't ever want to hear you say something like that again," Mom said. She had a hurt look in her eyes. But I could tell she saw how large I had gotten.

How couldn't she?

She just didn't have the heart to tell me.

Mom took the shirt from me and hung it back up. Then she walked out of the room. I heard her go into her bedroom. A few moments later she came back with a shirt of my dad's.

"Wear this."

It was my favorite T-shirt he owned. He had bought it years ago with me and her. We'd gone to New York.

I'd seen a booth on the street that had a bunch of fun stuff. Clothing, shot glasses, funny purses. The vendor told me I could choose any of the tees I wanted off his cart. Only five dollars. I'd picked this shirt and given it to Dad. It had a giant apple on it. I'd thought he would like it since he was a cook.

I took the shirt from Mom and threw it on over my tank top.

It still smelled a little like Dad.

"How ridiculous do I look?" I spun around for Mom to see.

She laughed. "You look like a girl in her father's shirt," she said.

"That's the look I was going for," I said.

Mom and I walked all over our small city that day. We went to the Dairy Queen where they always burned the fries. We walked to my high school. Mom showed me the bar where she'd had her first drink on her twenty-first birthday.

It was a good walk. And it lifted my spirits to the point where I started getting out of bed again.

Mom and I made it a habit.

Every morning we would walk. About six miles.

We'd talked about everything.

And sometimes nothing.

Some mornings Mom would cry, some I would. But it was nice just being with each other.

8

Souls

"Just remember what Charles told you. Let the souls come to you, because they will. Don't go out looking for your family, or for the souls, or for anything. Just get in and get out," Brandy says.

We talk outside of my "last spot" before I go back down to where the living are. I've gotten the rules from Charles drilled into my head.

Befriend nothing, and no one (including other Reapers).

Don't look for your family, or the souls.

Don't get attached to earth, because you're not going to be there long.

Never reveal yourself.

Keep the people Upstairs notified with your progress.

If the rules are broken you'll get bad marks, and bad marks

could mean extra souls, or harder souls to collect, like children and babies. Each rule has its own punishment. Sometimes they don't even tell you how you'll be punished.

A lot of it seems like a bluff. What more can they do to me? I'm already dead.

"I know," I say. I had to repeat them over and over again to Charles and the class. He picked on me, and I knew it was because of the interruption I had made. Even though that was his fault. If he hadn't picked on me, I wouldn't have said anything.

"You have to be careful. A lot of the girls forget who they are once they get there. It's very easy to slip back into your earthly ways. If that happens, it makes taking the souls a lot harder," Brandy says. She fixes my hair while she talks. I think she can tell I'm nervous.

I've never done something like this.

"Try not to touch anyone," Brandy says. "Remember what Charles told you. They won't always die, but you can still bring death to them or their loved ones."

"Or make them sick. I know. I don't want to touch anyone. I just want to get this over with," I say.

"Just don't forget," she says again.

I have no idea what to expect, and at the same time, I feel like this can't be real. It all still feels like a dream. A dream I can't escape from. One I'll never wake up from.

"How will I find Martha?" I ask.

Martha is one of the women the dead stay with while they do their work.

My mentor. But not only that, she also takes care of us. Feeds us. Gives us a place to sleep.

"How will I find her?" I start to feel panicked again. I know I should have worried about this before, but there was so much to worry about, I didn't have time.

"She's exactly where you want to be. Just walk and you'll find her. I promise. I'll be checking up on you too," Brandy says. She hands me a cell phone.

"Don't give that to anyone. It's a direct contact to me. It's expensive, so only call when you absolutely need me," she says. "And I'll send you messages every few days. Once you get your first soul, I'll send you the second, and instructions. All of the souls will be in the same area, so don't go out wandering."

Brandy leads me into the last room. The only thing in here is a dark chair with buttons on the armrest.

"This is the end of the line, Rosie. Are you ready?"

I glance around. None of it reminds me of my life before.

How can this be the end of the line? I thought maybe I would just ride a spaceship back down to earth.

"I don't know if I am," I say. Brandy grabs my hand and squeezes it. Then she leads me to the chair where I sit.

"That's the right answer," she says, then smiles. "You're going to do fine. Just remember the rules."

"What do I do now?" My voice shakes when I speak. Is this going to hurt? Am I going to be reborn? What if I don't wake up? What if this is all a trick?

"When I shut the door, just press that green button. Close your eyes, and count to ten. You'll be gone before you get to five," Brandy says. She backs out of the room as she speaks. She stands at the door and waves to me.

"I guess I'll see you on the other side," I say. Brandy laughs.

"Good luck, Rosie Wolfe." She walks out of the room and closes the door behind her.

I've never felt so frightened. I look down at the green button.

It just sits there. Waiting to be pushed.

Before I can touch it, the door to the room opens again.

"Rosie, I forgot to tell you. Your dad is fine. And he's waiting for you," Brandy says. She gives me a smile, and then leaves.

For good this time.

Dad is okay. And he knows I'm here. He knows I'll see him soon.

I have to get this over with.

Before I can talk myself out of it, I click the green button again. Then I shut my eyes.

One.

Two.

Three.

Four.

Five.

Si—

9

Earth

"Are you all right?"

I look, and a small child stands above me. He holds a melting chocolate ice cream cone. It drips down his hand.

"Miss, are you all right?" Another person comes into view. A middle-aged woman. She carries a small baby on her hip. She reaches her hand out for me.

I realize I'm on my back.

I look around.

There's bark under me, and my head feels like it's been hit by a bat.

The lady keeps her hand held out until I take it. She pulls me up. I glance around and see a set of swings, a red slide, and monkey bars.

I'm in a park.

The sun is hot and my eyes ache from how bright it is.

"You took a pretty big spill," the woman says.

She guides me to a bench not far from the swings. The child she carries smiles at me. A little girl in a pink tank top and yellow shorts. She looks like she's not even a year old.

"A spill?" I glance around.

Children play on the monkey bars. Laugh as they go down the red slide.

When kids laughed it was something Mom always liked. She said just hearing a kid laugh made her day that much better.

"Did you hit your head that hard? You fell off the swings. Should I call an ambulance?" the woman asks.

It takes me a moment to realize that I'm on earth again.

Was I on earth before?

I stand and dust myself off.

I'm a Reaper now.

The souls are here somewhere.

"I'm fine. Did you see where my bag went?" I know I was sent with a bag.

My first name.

Some clothes.

The woman nods and points to the swing set. A few feet behind it my bag sits.

"Thank you," I say.

I run over and grab the bag, pull out the letter, and check to make sure that my first soul isn't here.

Name: Martin Gables
Age: 64
Occupation: retired garbage collector

Interests: fishing, reading, yard work, etc.
Cause of death: stroke
Note:
You do not kill these humans.
All you have to do is touch them.
If you're an animal, rub against them somehow. Or if
you've returned as a bird, perch on their shoulder.
Just be subtle.
If you're going back as a human, somehow touch
them lightly on the shoulder. They will pass away a
few hours later.
Remember: If you don't touch them on the shoulder,
nothing will happen.
And be careful not to touch anyone else there. There are
consequences for interacting with souls that are not on
your list.
Be sure to contact someone Upstairs if a situation arises,
whether you've gone back as an animal or a human.
If you make a mistake, you may be punished with extra
souls, or more difficult souls to collect. It can also
jeopardize your chances of moving on.

I grab my bag and walk down the street. I don't see why an old man would stick around a park.

Maybe if he's a creep. But I think they would have told me if he were. Right?

Would Martha hang around a place like this? How will she find me? I don't even know what she looks like.

Does she know what I look like? Have they sent her pictures of the new me?

"Are you sure you're all right?" The woman has come back

over to where I am. Her cute baby still smiling.

"Yes, I'm fine. I think I just need to get some water. Thanks for checking." Then I walk away.

I pass small neighborhoods with more children who play on slides and climb trees, and families who walk their dogs.

I remember every summer. Dad hated how ugly the lawn turned.

The lawns here are dead and yellow. Just like in my old neighborhood.

What day is it?

I had no sense of time Upstairs. Could it be the same day as when I passed?

Who knows?

The weather feels the same as when I was on earth.

Upstairs, they didn't tell us much about time, or maybe I didn't think to ask.

From the looks of it not much has changed. The area even seems like the same kind of place I grew up in.

After a few minutes of walking I come up on a 7-Eleven.

I walk through the doors and a bell rings. I'm hit with the AC from inside and it makes me realize how hot it is out.

The store smells like hot dogs and burned coffee. I used to love the smell of these types of places, but today it makes my eyes and head hurt.

Everything on my body hurts.

So much for no more pain. I should have savored it while I had the chance.

"How's it going?" a man at the counter says. He gives me a nice smile when I walk inside.

I wave to him.

He has a frizzy beard and stretched earlobes. I think I'm the only customer here.

"Hi, uh, do you know what time it is? And what day?" I walk to the counter.

The man smiles again, and then pulls out his cell phone. A model of a phone I've never seen before. I glance at it, and then at the phone Brandy gave me. They look completely different.

"It's Wednesday, four thirty-five p.m. You from out of town? Just get off a plane?" he asks.

He looks down at my bag. It's a little larger than a purse. I guess I can see why he might think I'm not from around here.

He's right. I'm not.

"Yes, thank you," I say. I walk over to the Slurpees.

I watch the flavors turn in the machine. Blue Raspberry, Piña Colada, and Coke.

My favorite.

It's been almost a week since I died. I lost five whole days and didn't even know it. It felt like I'd been Upstairs for only a few hours. How could I have lost that much time?

My stomach growls at me.

I'm so hungry.

My mouth waters as I watch the Slurpees.

"You need directions to somewhere? Are you waiting for some-one to come get you?" the man asks.

He has a nice tone, but I think he might be suspicious of me. Or maybe I'm just overworrying.

"No, I, uh, I'm walking there now. I just stopped in to get some cool air. Thanks," I say, taking one last look at the Slurpees.

Why didn't Brandy send me down here with any money?

Even though I'm already dead, I feel like I could starve to death.

I guess I get to spend the rest of my time here. Hungry, uncom-fortable, and in pain.

Maybe being dead was better than this.

10

Martha

I walk down the street for hours.

Waiting for Martha to find me.

I'm tempted to call Brandy, but I know I shouldn't. I can't mess up. This has to be done perfect so I can get back to Dad.

Finally, as the sun is set and the air is getting cooler, a car stops next to the sidewalk.

The window on the passenger side rolls down. I see a young guy in the seat. He has black hair and tanned skin. He looks about my age. Maybe sixteen?

"Hey, are you all right?" he asks. I try to look past him to see who might be driving. What if it's Martha?

I can't see though. It's almost too dark out to see the boy who talks to me, let alone the driver.

"I'm fine," I say. Am I okay?

The later it gets the more disappointed I feel.

This whole thing has been so overwhelming. I'm all alone out here and I feel sort of forgotten.

What if I *have* been forgotten?

"You sure?" he asks.

He has a sweet tone. Like maybe he really is worried.

Is this a sign?

Is this Martha disguised as a young boy? If she was driving, wouldn't she get out and talk to me?

Brandy didn't tell me how Martha would find me. Just that she would.

Eventually.

How long do I have to wait for her? How long is eventually? It's been hours and I'm tired and alone. Not to mention I'm freaked out.

I didn't know ghosts got afraid.

Not ghosts. Reapers.

I keep forgetting. I'm not a ghost. Not that it even matters.

I walk up to the window and peek inside. The driver looks like he's a few years older than me. Similar to the boy who sits on the passenger side.

Same tanned skin. Same dark hair.

"Do you know where I am? I'm looking for a woman named Martha, but I don't know exactly where to find her," I say.

I glance up and down the streets. There aren't many people out here. This is a small and quiet town.

The house that I've stopped in front of has a pink bike in the front yard. It reminds me of something I rode years ago. Only my bike had tassels on the side.

"To be honest, I'm not even sure where I am," I say.

If these boys are serial killers, can they chop me up and throw me in a lake? Is it possible for me to die twice?

At least now I know I'll feel the pain, if they do decide to chop me up.

"Martha Blackburn? Does she have frizzy red hair?" When the driver says this, he leans in close to the window.

I shrug.

"I don't know what she looks like, I just know that she takes in a lot of guests, I guess," I say.

Is this how I'm supposed to find her?

Is this how my souls find me?

The boy by the window looks to the kid next to him.

"Martha who lives a few blocks from Mom? She does have a lot of guests this time of year." He turns to me. "We know where she lives. Just up the road a ways. Do you want a ride?"

They don't seem like a threat, but at the same time, this could be a mistake.

The serial killer thought pops into my head again. Where would they put my body? Bury me in a ditch?

For all I know I'm already buried somewhere else.

Before, the thought of getting in a car with strangers would have been out of this world. But I can't tell anymore. What's a sign and what isn't?

I hesitate for a minute longer, and then answer him.

"Are you sure you aren't going to kill me?" I ask. I know it sounds silly, but I say it anyway.

I don't know how the world is. What if in these last few days everyone's changed for the worse?

The driver throws his head back and laughs. The boy by the window gives me a big grin. For some reason his smile reminds me of my mother's.

Contagious.

"Cross my heart. We're not gonna hurt you. But if you'd rather walk, I can give you the address," he says.

I take that as a good sign and get into the car.

11

Carrie

"Carrie hasn't been very nice to you lately," Mom said.

We both sat on our front porch swing. Dad built it a few years ago for one of their anniversaries. Right before he got sick.

Mom sipped her iced tea after she said that. Then she looked over at me and gave me her *Mother knows best* look.

I knew what she was talking about, but that didn't mean I wanted to talk about it.

"Rosie, why don't you do something about it? Aren't best friends supposed to talk about these sorts of things?" Her tone was soft. Like she tried to tiptoe around the topic, even though she brought it up in the first place.

"Carrie's just weird," I said. I swung back and forth, faster than we had been earlier.

Talking about this made me nervous.

It was like when we talked about Dad. I wanted to avoid the topic. But somehow I knew I wasn't going to be able to.

"She hates that no one talks about her like they used to, doesn't she? Has she mentioned your father's death at all? Since the funeral?" Mom asked.

Sometimes it amazed me how much my mother knew. Even when I didn't talk about it, she knew.

Carrie hadn't asked me how I was doing since the funeral. She hugged me once, at the cemetery, and that was it. Since then she'd talked nonstop about herself, and when people asked me how I was doing, she would get annoyed. She'd even snap at her mom when she asked how I was doing.

In a town this small, it's hard to share attention. And a few years back, Carrie was the talk of the town, because her father ran off with another man.

"She just handles things different from me, I guess," I said.

How does anyone handle death, though?

I wasn't sure.

Mom and I hadn't had a choice. We just had to.

Carrie didn't have it on her doorstep, so I guess that meant she could ignore it. Ignore it until it came to get her, or someone she loved.

I wish it had been that easy for us.

"I don't want your best friend turning into a bully just because she doesn't get the attention that you get," Mom said. She sipped from her glass, and then handed it to me.

"Finish that for me, would you, honey?"

I took the cup from Mom and drank it. There was clearly vodka in it, but I drank it anyway.

These were the days when Mom was drinking. They didn't

last long, but she said it helped her sleep at night.

I didn't mind. Because after Dad passed, there were a lot of sleepless nights.

"Just remember, a best friend is supposed to lift you up, not drag you down. You've already had a hard enough few months. Don't make it harder on yourself, Rosie," Mom said. She sounded so tired.

So far away.

I felt bad that she had to talk to me about this sort of thing.

"I know, Mom. And I'm glad you're there for me," I said. Mom reached over and grabbed my hand.

I never knew she was my best friend until Dad died. And when he did, and it was just the two of us, I realized how lucky I was to have her around.

"I'll talk to Carrie," I said.

Mom nodded. "Maybe she's just handling this whole change differently. But talking will be good for you two. I don't want you to lose your best friend," she said.

It was so my mother. Worrying about my well-being. And happiness. And not worrying about her own.

12

Boys

I sit in the back of the car and wonder . . . is this breaking the rules?

Is this how Brandy wanted me to find Martha? Could I get into trouble?

"I'm Kyle, by the way," the kid in the passenger seat says. He leans back and holds out his hand to me.

Okay. As long as I don't touch his shoulder, he'll be okay.

He's not gonna die if I touch his hand, right?

That lady at the park didn't die, did she? She seemed all right.

Will someone she loves die because she touched me? Will she get sick?

I hesitate for a moment, and then shake his hand.

Instantly I feel a shock. I pull my hand away fast. He is still standing and doesn't seem to have felt the shock. I better not touch his shoulder. Not sure what would happen then.

I look at Kyle. He gives me a funny smile. "What's your name?" He must not have felt anything. And he isn't dead, so maybe handshakes are safe. The tingling in my hand starts to go away.

"Uh, I'm Rosie," I say.

"This is my older brother, Mitch," Kyle says.

Mitch says, "Hi," from the front seat, but continues to look forward while he drives.

"Where you from?" Kyle asks. He has a cheerful voice. Something Mom would call light.

Pleasant.

I don't know where I'm supposed to be from. Do I tell him where I was born? I can't say I'm from another world. That I'm from the grave.

"Around," I say. It sounds silly when I say it aloud, and I'm kind of embarrassed.

Kyle does his pleasant laugh again.

The backseat of the car is messy. There are old French fries on the floor and Big Gulp cups scattered around. It reminds me of Dad's car. He never cleaned it.

"That's all right. You don't have to tell me. Martha has a lot of visitors. I'm sure I'll get it out of you eventually," Kyle says.

"Stop it, Kyle, you sound like a creep," Mitch says. Then he laughs. Both boys talk and laugh similarly.

I wonder if I had had a sister, would she and I speak the same? Would people be able to tell we were related just by our laughs?

Mom told me she always wanted to have another girl, but her body struggled just with me.

I feel bad now, knowing that now she doesn't have a daughter or a husband.

I wonder how she's doing.

If she misses me.

Knows that I'm okay.

I wish so much that I could go and see her just to tell her that death isn't that bad. That I'll be seeing Dad soon and that he's happy.

Maybe I could have someone give her a letter for me.

Would she believe it was from me?

How could I get it to her?

"How long you in town for?" Kyle asks.

He brings me back to now. To this car.

This car with these two strangers who are taking me to meet another stranger.

It all seems so unreal.

But it feels so real.

"Until I get my work done. I'm here . . . for a job," I say. I try to sound chipper, but I suddenly don't know what I'm doing.

I miss Mom.

I miss Dad.

How long until I get to see them? Do I have to do this all alone?

How long does it all take?

What if it's years?

"You down here for the summer? A lot of people come to work at the waterpark. Is that where you're working at?" Kyle says. He talks a lot. Asks more questions than any boy I've ever met.

Is it because my skin is perfect and I'm almost a new person? Or is he different?

I wonder what my life would have been like if I had looked like

I do now. Would it have been easier? Would it have made any difference in the way everything turned out?

"Summer's almost over. Why would she start working there so late?" Mitch says.

Kyle nods. "I guess you're right."

He looks at me and waits for my answer.

I don't know if I have one.

"I'm just down here doing family stuff. Like a family job," I say. I glance out the window. We're in an older-looking neighborhood now. Kids play on the sidewalk and ride on their bikes. Even though it's dark out, they look like they are enjoying the last few weeks of the warm weather.

It reminds me of when I was younger and Dad taught me how to ride my pink bike. We'd stayed out until way past dark just so I could say I learned to ride on two wheels the first day. Mom sat in the grass next to the sidewalk and cheered us on.

"Well, Rosie, it's your lucky day, Kyle can't continue creeping you out. We're here," Mitch says.

We pull into a driveway of a house that is well lit up. There's a brown station wagon parked in front and lots of stuff scattered around the grass.

"This is Martha's?" I ask.

Both the boys nod.

"We live just down the road. Maybe I'll come and visit you," Kyle says. Then he gives me a big smile. He has really white teeth. His smile makes me want to smile, even though I don't feel happy.

"Okay," I say. I jump out of the car and walk up to the house. I turn and watch as the boys drive away.

13

Martha. Finally.

I don't know if I should knock, or ring the bell. There are windows on the side of the door. I peek inside. I don't see anyone. There's a big chandelier and a flight of stairs.

Is this really Martha's house?

Is it the right Martha?

Brandy told me to walk and I would find her. And that's mostly what I've done.

I take a few steps back and look at the house from afar. Even though it's old, it looks like a cozy place to live.

I glance at the side of the yard. A black cat sits and stares at me.

Is that cat a Reaper?

"Hey! Are you a Reaper?" I walk over to the cat. It stands there for a second more and then runs away.

"Come back!" I shout.

I walk back over to the window and peek in again.

If that cat was a Reaper, would it stay in the house with me? Would I know?

I look in the windows, trying to find a litter box. Before I know it the front door opens.

"What do you think you're doing?" a woman says.

She's fat, with carrot-colored frizzy hair. She looks like what I imagine Little Orphan Annie would grow up to be like.

She holds a spatula in one hand, and has the other on her hip.

"Wha? Sorry, I . . ." I hesitate for a minute.

She stares at me. Probably waiting for my response. My excuse for being a Peeping Tom.

A Reaping Tom. Ha ha ha.

"I didn't know anyone was home," I say.

Even though there's a car in the driveway and the lights are on. No need to mention that.

"Did you bother to ring the doorbell?" She points to the doorbell with the spatula.

As she speaks, I notice the smell of cooking coming from the house. It smells like something Dad used to make on Christmas.

A pot roast.

My stomach grumbles. I don't think I've ever gone this long without eating.

I guess having a dad who cooked spoiled me.

"I'm sorry. I'm not sure what to do. Are you Martha?"

She gives me a funny look and then steps a little closer.

"You broke the rules, you broke the rules. Do you know how much trouble you could get in? Inside, before someone notices you're here," she says. She hustles me into the house and slams the door, and locks it behind her.

The foyer to the house is well lit by the chandelier that hangs above me. The floors are cherrywood and the walls are painted a cream color.

This place *is* cozy.

"I didn't know where you were. I was walking for hours. How long were you going to leave me out there?" I try to hide my anger as I speak to her.

What did this woman expect from me?

To sleep on the streets?

In the gutter?

Maybe she wanted me to stay at the 7-Eleven with the man and the Slurpee machines.

"I would have come for you, but you didn't give me a chance. Just come inside. Tell me no one knows you're here," Martha says. She walks into her kitchen. There is a huge table that could probably seat a dozen people.

She walks to the fridge and pulls out a bottled water and hands it to me. Then she stands in front of the stove and stirs a pot. I hear something boil inside it.

I ignore her question, and try to change the subject.

"How did you know it was me? Who and when did the people above tell you I was coming?" I open my water and take a long sip. The water is nice to have, but my stomach needs food.

"They always tell me, I just wish you had followed the rules and stayed where you were. The real question is how did you find me?" Martha pulls a bowl out of one of the cabinets and fills it with soup. Then she hands it to me.

"I guess I just stumbled on the house. I was out walking for hours. I saw a black cat out there. Is that another Reaper?" I don't look at her when I say this.

The soup smells amazing and makes my mouth water. Martha hands me a spoon and I take a bite.

It reminds me of being with Mom and Dad.

Again I wonder how Mom's doing.

Where she is.

If she misses me.

What if I called her, just to check in? To hear her voice. Would that get me into trouble? I know without having to ask that that has to be against the rules.

Even though I know she misses me. I feel awful that she's been left here alone. Without me or Dad.

"You think I could take two of you in at a time? You've been here ten minutes and already you're a pain in my ass. I can't imagine dealing with two at once," Martha says.

That doesn't really answer my question about the cat. But now I'll never look at any animal the same. They're probably all Reapers. Out to take the living. Out to trick us into dying.

Martha walks around the counter. "Tell me the truth, Rosie Wolfe. How did you find me?" She sits down, then gives me one of those *don't mess with me* faces. I guess there isn't any point in lying so I tell the truth.

"The boys across the street. I asked if they knew you, and they took me here. But I promise I didn't tell them anything."

Martha gives a huge sigh. Then puts her hand on her face.

"The Morales boys? Rosie, you could get in a lot of trouble for that. If Brandy finds out, she will have to report it. I won't say anything. Just don't let that sort of thing happen again. Don't you want easy souls? Don't you want to get this over with?" she says. Then she gets up and pulls a carton of ice cream out of the freezer.

"I don't want any souls, so what difference does it make?"

Is taking the soul of an old, lonely man any different from taking someone my own age?

"Eat your soup, have a bowl of ice cream, then go to bed. We have a lot to talk about tomorrow," she says.

But I can't stop thinking about that boy.

"I touched Kyle's hand. Does that mean he's going to die?" I ask.

Martha sighs. "Did you touch his shoulder?"

I think about that feeling I got when I shook his hand. He was so cute, and so nice.

"No, just his hand," I say.

I can tell Martha is already sick of me, but I need to know. I don't want him to die because of me.

"I highly doubt it, Rosie. He might get sick, but he won't die. Just don't touch anyone else."

I'm surprised that that's all she says.

After I eat the ice cream, Martha walks me upstairs and shows me where my room is. Before I can say good night she closes the door behind her.

I'm asleep right when my head hits the pillow.

14

Birthday

"Your dad wants to try making duck this year," Mom said. We both walked around the grocery store and looked for stuff to cook.

It was Dad's birthday. He always made special meals on birthdays. Including his own. But this year, he was so sick Mom wasn't sure he was going to be able to.

"Duck? Why did he decide on that?" I put a bag of lettuce in the cart.

Mom shrugged. "I guess he's been watching a lot of those cooking shows again. Wants to try something new."

Dad hadn't been back to work in over two months. He was the head chef at a fancy restaurant a few miles from our house. But since the chemo took most of his energy, he stayed at home and watched cooking shows.

I could tell it made him sad watching people cook instead of doing it himself.

I hated seeing him that way.

He'd even stopped writing his cookbooks.

"I don't think he's gonna be able to make anything, let alone a duck," I said.

Mom pushed the cart toward the dairy section. She put milk, eggs, and whatever else in the basket.

"Don't say that, Rosie. He might have the energy." She didn't sound that convinced when she said this.

"Where do we even buy a duck? I doubt they have them sitting at the deli." I put a gallon of chocolate milk in the cart.

Chocolate milk for Dad's pills.

"We could run over to that organic place. I hear they have some interesting food. I don't know, Rosie. I just want your dad to be happy." When Mom said this, she started to cry.

These were the days when she would spill her tears over just about anything. Especially if it involved Dad.

I glanced around the store to see if anyone noticed Mom's tears. A lady walked past us pushing her cart with a little girl sitting in it. The girl gave me a big smile. Her hair was pulled back into two pigtails. I could tell the lady was trying not to stare at Mom.

"Don't cry. I promise, what Dad makes isn't going to change his mood. Let's just get him the usual steak and help him cook it," I said. I patted Mom on the shoulder.

We walked out of the store, loaded our car with the groceries, and drove home. It was getting dark when we pulled into the driveway. I looked at the house and noticed all the lights were shut off.

"Is Dad not here?"

It wasn't like Dad to leave the lights off. In case something happened and we needed to find him.

Mom jumped out of the car and left the food behind her.

I followed.

She stumbled around, looking for her key.

I grabbed my set and unlocked the door. When we got inside everything was quiet and dark.

"Dad?" I yelled. I could hear Mom's panicked voice behind me, even though I know she didn't want me to notice.

I was worried too.

"Hello?" Mom shouted, turning on the lights to the foyer and living room.

"Do you think something happened?" I said to Mom.

She ignored me and called Dad's name again.

"Josh!"

I saw a small light coming from the kitchen when I heard Dad's voice.

"I'm in here." He sounded hurt.

"Oh no, Josh. Are you okay?" Mom said. We both ran into the kitchen.

Dad sat at the table, grinning. There were candles, and three places set for us to eat. On the table was a beautiful meal.

"Surprise," Dad said. He walked over to us and put his arms around me and Mom.

"I made the duck." Dad pointed to the meat at the center of the table.

It all looked gorgeous. Better than any of those chefs on TV could make. And it smelled amazing.

"Dad, did you make this alone?" I flicked on the lights. I couldn't believe it.

Where did he get the energy? His body was frail. He looked like he could have dropped dead right then. Even his skin hung off him.

But I hadn't seen him look that happy in a long time. Since before he had gotten sick.

"I wanted to do something big for my last birthday," Dad said. When he said this, it felt like someone had stabbed me in the heart. I looked at Mom. She looked worse than I felt.

"Don't ever say that again," Mom said.

Dad laughed like it was the funniest joke in the world.

Mom ignored Dad's laughter and served us each a plate of food.

Dad sat at the head of the table.

It was the best thing I'd ever eaten.

Better than Christmas dinners at Dad's restaurant, better than all my birthdays combined. He outdid himself.

At the end of dinner, Dad got sick and had to lie down. But that didn't stop him from eating dessert with us.

"Bring it in here . . . ," he said from his room. Mom opened the fridge and pulled out three perfect chocolate mousses.

We all sat around Dad's bed and talked about memories. Of life before. Before all the pills, and chemo, and doctors.

We also talked about our lives together.

About me going to school in a few years.

About Dad opening up new restaurants in different cities.

About Mom writing her own cookbook.

Our future.

Our future together, that we all knew we couldn't really have.

15

Getting to Work

"Rosie, time to get up. Rosie. Right now."

I open my eyes to see Martha staring at me. She wears an apron on it that says KICK-ASS COOK and holds yet another spatula. Dad used to have an apron like that. Mom and I had bought it for him for Father's Day years ago. Somehow it fits Martha's personality, though.

"Why can't I sleep?" I pull the blanket up to my chin. It's soft and light. Like a blanket of clouds. I could lie in this bed forever. I haven't slept that well in a long time. Like I was transported to a different world.

"You've been asleep for thirteen hours. It's time to get up," she says. Then walks out of the bedroom.

I sit up and look at the alarm clock next to the bed. 11:43 a.m. Wow, I did sleep for a long time.

I get out of bed and make my way to the bathroom. When I open the door to my room I'm hit with the smell of bread.

Cinnamon rolls.

I hurry into the bathroom to wash my face.

When I look at myself in the mirror I'm surprised. I forgot about my freckles. And hair. That sleep almost brought me back to my old life.

Almost.

I take a quick shower, and head downstairs.

Martha meets me as I walk into the kitchen.

"Hungry?" She pours a glass of milk and hands it to me with a roll. Then she whips up a bowl of oatmeal and slides it across the counter.

Oatmeal.

Something Dad used to eat all the time.

"It's good for the brain," he'd say. He would put raisins in mine, and a little sugar. But that didn't change the texture, which I hated.

"Thank you." I take a bite of the cinnamon roll. It's like nothing I've ever tasted before. The frosting melts in my mouth, and the flavor is rich and creamy, with a little spice to it.

"This is amazing." I want more. Five more. I could probably eat a whole pan of these. If everything Martha cooks is half as good as this, then I'll be back to my old self in days.

I look at the counter where Martha has set the pan of cinnamon rolls. There's at least a dozen there.

Would she notice if I took two more? Three more?

"You still have to eat the oatmeal." Martha points to the bowl she's just set down.

There aren't any raisins in the oatmeal. It doesn't look like there's sugar or milk in it either. I take a bite and it's the exact opposite of the roll.

"Do you have any sugar?" I ask.

Martha folds her arms. She looks at me like she wants to give me a good slap on the head.

"Isn't the roll sweet enough? Just eat the damn oatmeal, Rosie. Beggars can't be choosers," she says. She turns her back to me and starts a pot of coffee. Then she walks over and sits next to me.

"I'm sorry. I've been told I need to watch my tone with the new Reapers. It's just been a rough week," she says.

It's not my fault I'm here. I bet if she were in my position she'd be a lot angrier.

"It's okay." I take another bite of the oatmeal. It slides down my throat and makes me want to throw up. I don't even think sugar would make this stuff taste better.

"Are you dead too?" I try to distract myself from the taste. Martha bursts out laughing and shakes her head.

"Hell, no! They had a job posting online, and at first I didn't believe it, but after the interview, and a bunch of other stuff I can't talk about, I believed them," Martha says. She gets up, walks over to the cabinet, and pulls out a pack of cigarettes. She takes one out and lights it.

Smoking in the house?

"That will give you cancer," I say, looking down at my plate.

"Everything gives you cancer, Rosie. And whatever kills me the fastest, right?" she says, and then laughs again.

For some reason when she says this I want to cry.

Dad didn't smoke. Neither did I. Sometimes Mom would sneak a smoke here and there after Dad passed away. But not a lot.

"Smoking isn't the only thing that will give you cancer," I say.

Martha inhales, and then blows out a big smoke ring. Then she coughs.

I slide my roll and oatmeal across the counter to her.

"I'm not hungry anymore," I say. The smell of the smoke and the thought of Dad, and Mom all alone, ruin it for me. I don't even want to finish the roll. I just want to get this job over with and leave.

No one Upstairs warned me about emotions. For some reason my emotions are so much stronger now. And up and down. I feel like I've fallen in the pit of despair one minute, and the next like maybe I'm floating on clouds.

"What's wrong? Did you die of cancer? Oh, honey, I'm sorry," Martha says. She runs her cigarette under the tap. Then walks over and pats me on the back.

"Being dead is the best thing that happened to you. Still, I'm sorry. You're so young. Cancer? Geez," she says. Before she can finish I cut her off.

"I didn't die of cancer. My dad did. A year ago," I say. My voice comes out harsh and annoyed.

I know it's rude, and I know I shouldn't be, but all of this . . . the death of everything. It's almost too much for me to handle.

How many people who die ask why? Say it isn't fair? Am I the first?

"Oh," Martha says. She gets up, takes my bowl, and dumps the remaining food in the trash.

"You don't have to finish that," she says. Then she does a big sigh. "You know, I've had forty-two Reapers come in and out of my house, and every story makes me sad in a different way. I still can't learn to detach myself from the emotions, I'm sorry." When Martha says this, I feel bad for her.

Like I've hurt her.

That small bit of my story made her feel a little bit of my pain.

I don't want anyone to feel my pain.

"It's okay. Have you ever had anyone you love die?" I ask.

Martha nods. "Just about everyone in my family. That's why I took the job. If I help a hundred Reapers, I'll be able to pass on and see my family. Without having to go through the reaping business myself."

Different jobs for different people.

I wish I could have gotten a different job.

But I don't have this beautiful house, or anywhere to keep Reapers. Or souls. Or whatever.

And I guess I'd have to be alive.

Martha's kitchen is shiny and new. It looks like something Mom would have had in her dream home. Hardwood floors, granite countertops, brand-new appliances.

Did they choose Martha because of her fancy home?

"How come some people get that option and others don't?" I ask.

"You're dead, Rosie. You wouldn't get this as a job."

Martha runs some hot water in the sink across from the counter. Then she fills it with soap. The smell reminds me of Mom.

Mom washing the dishes after breakfast. Lunch. Dinner. And even just to pass the time. To get her mind off things, she told me once.

"I took this job by choice. This house isn't cheap. Plus, the people who die young don't get many options. Death would prefer to send out fresh souls to do her reaping. The people who die old get other jobs, or options, or whatever. I don't know all the details," Martha says. "And to be honest, the ones who die young are lucky. Trust me. I've heard some horror stories about the jobs for the old. That being said, let's get you to work. Meet me in the front yard in ten minutes."

"What kind of horror stories?"

Martha sighs. "It doesn't matter. But it's almost noon. We should have been out looking for your soul at ten. So go change. Scoot," she says.

I go upstairs to get my phone and name.

Name: Martin Gables
Age: 64
Occupation: retired garbage collector
Interests: fishing, reading, yard work, etc.
Cause of death: stroke

Just reading his name makes chills run through my body.
Like he's haunting me.
Martin Gables has to die today, all because of me.

16

Breaking Rules

"What they don't tell you Upstairs is some of the rules must be bent a little bit," Martha says.

We both sit outside in her front yard. The day is a hot one.

Martha's yard has long grass and is covered in weeds. It looks like it hasn't been mowed in over a year. I imagine it growing and turning into a huge forest, where all the Reapers hunt for their living prey.

Martha says learning the rules outside gives you a better feel for your surroundings. She points out bugs, animals, passersby— and tells me to imagine them all as souls as we talk. She says it makes things easier.

It's a little before one in the afternoon and I'm already sweating. Even though Martha's grass hasn't been cut, it's the only lawn on the whole street that hasn't died and turned that ugly yellow color.

"Like what?" I think about how mad she was when I broke a rule last night.

Getting a ride from those boys.

The Morales boys.

Both of them were so cute.

"Well, for one thing, if you had come back as a dog, do you think people would let just any dog into their house? No. So you have to get them to know you at least a little bit. Same as if you were to come back as a human. Or a cat. From what I've gathered, it's easiest when you're a bird," she says. She points to a cat that hides in the grass in her neighbor's yard. Is that the same cat as last night?

I hadn't even noticed it hiding there until she pointed it out.

Is it a Reaper?

Or is it just a regular cat?

I never liked cats growing up. They always seemed so stuck-up and snooty. I wanted to get a dog, but then Dad died, and pets were the last thing on my mind.

"See that cat? Would you let that into your house?" The cat looks like it's stalking something. Maybe its breakfast. Or maybe it's just trying to catch a bug.

"No, I'm allergic and my mom hates cats," I say. Plus, it could be a Reaper.

How deceptive the whole thing is.

Martha looks at me, and then rolls her eyes.

"Okay, well, what if you saw that cat for a few days, and it came into your yard with a hurt leg. Would you help it then?" Martha asks.

I think about how Mom rescued a dog once. We saw it cross the street and get hit. Mom stopped traffic just to get out and save the dog. Its two back legs were broken. I was certain it wasn't going to make it, but Mom reassured me that the dog would live. And sure enough, it did. We even returned it to its owner.

"I guess if it was hurt I probably would. Except I bet that cat is a Reaper. All the strays around here are, aren't they?" I say.

Is that how death caught Dad? Did they linger around for two years until taking him? Slowly getting him sicker and sicker?

"That cat is not a Reaper," Martha says. Although when I look at her, I can't tell if she's lying or not.

"Anyway. You noticed the cat. And if that cat was hurt, I'm sure you would help it out. Even though technically, in the rules, you're not supposed to be noticed. But no one is going to just approach some random cat," Martha says.

I try to think back to when I found out Dad had cancer.

Was there an animal that came around? Had it stayed with us? I can't think of anything. Mom didn't like pets, and Dad wouldn't have allowed just any stray into the house.

Had it gotten him while he was at work?

"A white dog took me. I guess I did notice it. The dog hung around a few days before I died," I say aloud. More to myself than Martha.

I should have just let the dog die in the road. Avoided death all together. But if I hadn't saved the dog, what would it have done to the Reaper?

All these questions are making my brain feel fuzzy. I hate it.

"See, that's how you have to break the rules. The soul has to know you're there. Otherwise, you can't take them," Martha says.

"Are you sure that cat isn't a Reaper?" I point to the kitty. It looks like it's creeping closer and closer to us, but I could just be imagining things.

"If it is, it's none of our business. All right, let's take a walk and find where your souls live," Martha says. She walks toward the road.

I get up and follow her. "Where do the other Reapers stay? Are there more people like you?"

There must be hundreds of us. Millions of us.

How many people die a day?

A week?

"Yes, but I don't know who or where they are," Martha says. She leads me down the driveway.

This neighborhood reminds me of somewhere my grandparents live.

Lawns with little flowers planted at the edges. White fences. Bird feeders.

"What state are we in?" I ask. I hadn't even thought about that until now. I haven't thought about a lot of stuff until now.

How long is this going to take?

What if I can't do it?

What if I don't do it right and they punish me?

Martha continues to walk. "It doesn't matter where we are. Just do your job."

I guess it really doesn't matter. It's not like I can go out and explore anyway. I have to get this done.

Then I can leave and find Dad.

17

Finding Martin

"**That's Martin's house,**" Martha says. We both stand outside a little brown house. It looks haunted and old. It has a beat-up car in the driveway. The yard has trash scattered all around it.

"He's inside?" I walk around the yard. Coke bottles, old cartons of cigarettes, McDonald's wrappers. What's left of the grass is yellowed and dead. The total opposite of Martha's grass.

"I'd assume so. I know he doesn't have a job," Martha says.

"Do you know him?" I ask.

He lives just a few blocks from Martha. If he lived that close to Mom, she would have made it a point to get to know him. Especially if he lived alone, and didn't have a wife or children.

"I've seen him out walking a few times. He isn't the friendliest person," she says. "I said hi to him once, and he blew me off. I was surprised when you told me he was the first name on your list. I thought this guy would live forever," she says.

Martha stands on the sidewalk, near Martin's yard, but not on the grass. She has her arms crossed. The breeze blows her fluffy hair all over the place, but she doesn't seem to notice or care.

"Then should I knock on his door?" I take a few steps closer to the front door.

"What? No. Rosie, get back here. We both know that's not how this works," Martha says. She sounds angry, and looks even angrier.

I go back to where she stands. She turns from me and walks toward her house.

"Why would you think you could knock on the door with me standing right here? Are you trying to blow both our covers?" she says. For the large woman that she is, she moves at a faster pace than I would have thought.

Martha rants to me as we head back to her place. I notice what must be Kyle and Mitch's house as we head back.

The boys from last night.

Kyle sits in his front yard with a young girl. She looks like she's about four years old. They play catch together. I can't help but stare.

When he sees me, he waves.

"Hey. Mystery chick." He holds the hand of the little girl and crosses the street to where Martha and I walk.

"Great," Martha says under her breath. But loud enough for me to hear.

She's one grumpy lady.

"Hi," I say. My voice comes out louder than I plan and I feel my face go hot.

Just stay calm.

I can talk to this boy without panicking.

"How's the trip been so far? I see Martha found you. How are you doing?" Kyle looks at Martha. She gives him a big grin. Then glances at me. Her eyes don't look happy, even though the rest of her does.

Some people you can just tell. Angry eyes.

"I'm doing fine. Thanks for giving Rosie a ride last night, but we don't have much time to chat. She's got a lot of work to do."

He gives me another one of those contagious grins. "Well, Rosie, this is Penny, my little sister," Kyle says. The little girl waves and then hides her face. She's so cute that I can't pretend like I don't know she's there. She has dark hair like her brothers. It's braided with a pink bow at the end.

"Hi, Penny," I say.

"Do you think you'd wanna come play some catch with Penny and me tonight after you're done with your work?" Kyle asks. He looks at Martha, maybe to ask permission? I don't know. She just shrugs at him, but gives me a look that says *you know better*.

I pause before I answer.

Will this keep me from seeing Dad?

I can't be rude, dead or not. I have to be polite.

Kyle is one of the cutest boys ever to have talked to me.

I nod without another thought. "I'd love to," I say. Maybe what I need is human contact.

Martha clears her throat. I look up at her. "It's time to go now, Rosie," she says. Then she walks ahead of me.

"She's not very happy, is she," Kyle says. "Oh well, just come on over whenever you're free. We'll look forward to it, won't we, Penny?" Kyle looks down at his little sister. She gives me a small smile and nods.

"Cool," I say. And then run to catch up with Martha.

A boy asked me to hang out.

A cute boy!

Dead or alive, I can't help but feel a little excited.

18

Carrie

"If you want guys to talk to you tonight, you have to do something about your hair, Rosie," Carrie said. We both sat on my bedroom floor in front of my body mirror. Carrie had a face of gorgeous makeup on, and her hair was done perfect. As usual. She'd been watching those YouTube makeup channels a lot and had been going full-blown face paint lately. Of course it still looked perfect on her.

Everything about her was perfect. And probably still is.

Everything but her attitude.

"My mom said I look the best when I wear my hair down, and curly," I said. I looked at myself in the mirror. We were getting ready for a bonfire Carrie's friends were having. She said there were going to be a lot of cool people there, and maybe even a few guys.

I hadn't looked this bad ever. I'd gained weight, my skin was broken out, and my hair was out of control.

But I didn't care about that sort of stuff. After Dad had died, it all seemed pointless.

"Rosie, what does your mom know? She's like sixty," Carrie said, then laughed.

Mom was in her forties, but I guess that doesn't make much of a difference to a teenager. At least not a teenager like Carrie.

"Here," Carrie said. She grabbed the hairbrush and ran it through my hair. Then leaned over and turned my straightener on.

I only straightened my hair on special occasions. The last time I'd done it was for Christmas last year.

Carrie straightened small sections of my hair. Then ran the brush through it. By the time she was finished my locks were silky and soft.

"Wow, I didn't know my hair was so long." I ran my fingers through it. Most of the time I just brushed it or pulled it back. And when I had used the flat iron, it never looked this good.

"Looks nice. Now let's see if that gets you a boyfriend easier than the frizz-ball hair you had before," Carrie said, then laughed.

I knew that she was joking, but it still stung a little bit.

Dad loved my hair when it was curly.

I stood up, and tried not to think about Dad. Or my hair. Or Carrie.

"Do you have a tank top you could throw on?" Carrie stared at my clothes. I wore cutoff shorts and a baggy T-shirt. I couldn't fit into any tight clothes anymore. Knowing I didn't fit in almost all of my old clothes made me want to scream.

"I won't wear a tank top," I said. Carrie burst out laughing. Then she walked over and put her arms around me. It made me feel hot and like my head might explode.

"Rosie, you're grieving. That looks fine. I just want people to notice you, that's all." Carrie was so good at bringing me down and lifting me up that half the time I wasn't sure if she was paying me a compliment or stabbing me with an insult.

"Let's just try to have a good time," I said.

When we got to the bonfire, I felt so out of place. It was the first time I'd left the house to do something social since Dad passed away.

Right when we walked in the door, people gave the sad face. Girls I'd never even spoken to came and hugged me. "I'm sorry about your dad, if you need anything just call me, okay?"

"I heard about your dad, such a bum deal. If you need someone to talk to just let me know."

Cute girls, cute boys, people on the football team, everyone. They all talked to me. Knew who I was.

And Carrie sat back and watched. She had a mean look on her face. Like she was angry. Or jealous.

Even when we were out by the fire, people still had something to say to me.

After what felt like the millionth person, Carrie shouted at me. She stood across the fire pit and used her "bitchy" tone.

"Why are you ignoring me, Rosie? I thought we were best friends. Why aren't you hanging with me?" she said. A few people looked at her, confused, and then at me, with pity.

I took a few steps back from the fire. The heat just added to my panic.

A boy next to me who was playing a guitar stopped and looked up at me. I felt myself start to sweat.

"What?" I don't know why I said this. Carrie walked around the fire pit and stood next to me.

"I'm the one who invited you and you totally blow me off like you don't even know me," Carrie said. She folded her skinny arms across her chest. Even in her anger, and with her mean face, she was still pretty.

I felt like a sad and sweaty girl looking at her.

"I'm not ignoring you. I just don't want to be rude. People were talking to me," I said. I looked around for help. Maybe someone could defend me. But no one did.

Everyone just stood and watched. I could tell the people around us felt uncomfortable.

A girl who had hugged me earlier walked into the house with a few of her friends. "Awkward," one of them said in a loud voice.

She was right. It was awkward.

"Well, did you forget that I was here?" Carrie said. She now used a voice that I'd heard her use with her mom. Something to get her mom to feel sorry for her.

I hated that voice. And it didn't work for me. I would have preferred her bitchy tone over it any day.

"No, how could I have forgotten? You've been giving me dirty looks since we got here. I swear you try to be mad at me," I said, surprised that I'd even defended myself.

Carrie stood in front of me and glared. She glanced around.

After a minute or two she walked away.

I stood there, not knowing what to do.

Guitar Boy started to play again.

One of the girls from my gym class approached me. "Carrie is a bitch. I don't know why you spend time with her," she said. Then she walked away too.

After a while I ended up going home alone.

Alone and sad.

I hadn't wanted to fight with Carrie. Or talk about Dad. Or any of it. I just wanted to have a good time. Or for a boy to like me, and for people to want to hang out. Not because they felt sorry for me, but because maybe we had something in common.

But that wasn't the case.

19

Angry Cooking

When we get back to the house, Martha is pissed off.

Again.

She wasn't kidding when she said she needed to work on her attitude toward the new Reapers.

"What do you think you're doing? You can't just become friends with one of the living. Rosie, what if someone Upstairs finds out about that?" Martha walks around her kitchen, takes stuff out of her fridge, and slams it on the counter.

It's like she's cooking, but angry cooking.

Dad used to do that.

Before he got sick, when he would get in arguments with me or Mom. It always produced a great meal.

"I didn't want to be rude," I say. I know it's a terrible excuse, but I've never had such a cute boy talk to me.

I don't tell Martha this, though.

"You didn't want to be rude? Right. Well, Rosie, this may sound rude, but I don't care. You can't talk to someone like that. You can't expect to have a *friendship* with someone. You're dead!" Martha shouts. As she talks, she cracks eggs into a bowl. She's moving so fast I don't know how she doesn't get a shell or two in.

Then she whips the eggs.

I bet she wishes she could whip me instead of those innocent eggs.

"I'm sorry, I am. I won't do it again." I don't know if that's true. Maybe I do want to go over and talk to that boy. Just for a little bit. To feel normal again.

Martha turns on the stove, and it makes the kitchen heat up. I sweat a little bit. That's something I missed when I was Upstairs.

No pain, and no smelly pits.

I change the subject. "Just forget about it. Can you please tell me what I'm supposed to do about Martin?"

When I mention his name, Martha seems to relax a little bit. Though the thought of him makes me feel anything but relaxed.

She pulls out a pan and puts it on the stove. She then puts butter in the pan. She throws in the beaten eggs, and then adds mushrooms, pepper, and onions to the mix. It smells like breakfast.

"What are you cooking?" I ask after she ignores my first question. She pulls ham out of her fridge and puts it in the eggs. Then folds the eggs over into an omelet.

"Comfort food. You're stressing me out, Rosie Wolfe," she says. She tastes the food in the pan. The look on her face makes me think she must like it. I stand up, go to the fridge, and pull out cheese. She has all sorts. I grab the goat cheese and mozzarella.

"Every omelet needs cheese." I sprinkle some in the pan and watch it melt. Then I add salt and pepper.

"You forgot to add that," I say, smiling. Martha gives me an annoyed face, but with a little bit of a smile.

"You like to cook?" she says.

I nod, and then taste the food.

It's amazing.

"Before my dad died he was a professional chef. We cooked all the time. You're almost as good of a cook as he is," I say.

Before he died I hated to cook.

But then toward the end of my life, I guess I learned to love it. I don't tell Martha that, though.

Martha laughs. "Almost? I doubt that. You mean he was almost as good of a cook as me," she says. She seems relaxed now.

The kitchen must be her happy place. It's warm with the stove on. But the smell of the food makes things comfortable.

Talking about food. Cooking.

"I'll admit that your cinnamon rolls are better," I say. Dad's were good, but Martha's were the best I've ever had. I feel a little guilty saying it aloud, but it's true.

Martha smiles. "I guess I'll take it." She pulls the omelet off the pan and cuts it in half, then puts it on two bright red plates.

"Let's eat. Then you can go take care of Martin."

Take care of Martin. The thought scares me.

But I ignore it and eat lunch.

It's delicious.

20

Martin

I stand at Martin's front door. I look around at his trashed yard. It's like people just walk past and throw their garbage on his lawn. He has weeds almost to my knees.

Martha says he only comes out in the evening to walk his dog. She's only spoken to him a few times, and has never noticed him have visitors. That's why I have to take him soon. Otherwise, he will die alone in his house, and no one will find him for a long time.

No one deserves to be forgotten for days.

But it happens. According to Martha people are forgotten because Reapers aren't doing their job right.

I don't want that to happen to Martin, so here I am.

Before I get too scared, I ring the doorbell. It takes a little while for Martin to open the door.

"Hello," he says. He's a short man with almost no hair. He looks a lot older than he is. He wears dirty pants and a button-up shirt. His voice is raspy and sounds tired. Next to his feet is an old dog. She's a black lab with a white chest and white paws. When she looks up at me, it's almost like she's smiling.

"Hi, are you Martin Gables?" I ask, even though I already know that he is.

Martin opens the door and waves me in. His dog makes a small sigh and walks into the house.

Is this allowed? Do I go in there?

I decide to just follow him. What's the harm? I'm not the one who's about to die.

"Sit down, please. Would you like something to drink?" he asks. I look around his house. It's spotless. Nothing like his yard outside. Completely remodeled with nice dark leather couches and a big-screen TV. I sit down on one of the couches. The old dog crawls up next to me. I make sure to sit far away from it. Will an animal die if I touch it?

Martin walks out of the room and into the kitchen, and then comes back in with a can of soda and a glass of what looks like whiskey.

Dad used to drink whiskey. But only after a long day at work, or on special occasions.

"Her name's Dolly, she loves visitors." He hands me the soda, then sits down on the couch next to me. He moves slowly, like everything on his body hurts. And when he sits, he grunts.

"How old is she?" I wonder why he hasn't asked me my name. Or who I am.

Does this man have dementia or something?

"About as old as you are," he says, looking at the dog.

I clear my throat, not sure what to say, or how long I should wait before taking this man's soul.

I look around the room. There are nice paintings on the wall. One of a mother holding her baby. Another is a framed picture of Dolly. Only she looks a lot younger. Almost a puppy.

"I know who you are," he says, still looking at the dog. He takes a sip of his drink, then makes a face like it's the worst thing in the world.

If it's whiskey, it *is* the worst thing in the world. I tried Dad's a few times. Made me wanna throw up every time I had even a little sip.

"You do?" I ask, not sure if he thinks I'm someone he knows or if he was expecting a visitor and maybe he thinks I'm her.

"You're here to end my life."

When he says this, I want to gasp.

How could he know?

Have I been that obvious?

Brandy is gonna kill me. Martha is gonna kill me. Even worse than kill me, not let me move on.

I stand up fast. The dog jumps. I drop my can of soda and spill it on the floor.

"Oh no," I say. I to try to clean it up with my shirt.

The panic is starting to set in.

Breathe.

Breathe.

"Relax, sit back down," Martin says. He gives me a small smile. I don't know why, but I do as he says and sit back on the couch. The dog gets up and licks the spilled soda off the carpet.

"I've been waiting for you since my daughter died. I'm glad you're here," he says.

He wants to die?

His daughter died?

So did Mom's.

"How did you know I was a Reaper?" I look down at the old dog. Dolly.

She looks up at me and gives me another one of her doggy smiles. I wish I had a dog like Dolly when I was alive. She looks like she'd be a good friend to have.

Even a best friend.

"I've seen Reapers before, and I've been waiting for mine for almost twenty years," he says, then takes another drink. The glass he drinks from is almost empty.

But I'm not like other Reapers. I'm human.

How could he know?

"I'm sorry about your daughter," I say. I can't help but wonder that this might be a test. Maybe the first soul is a test from Upstairs, to make sure we can do it?

Somehow I know that's not true. This man has seen stuff. I can tell.

He has a faraway look in his eyes when he speaks. Maybe it's the alcohol. Or maybe it's just him.

"It's all right. I'm just ready to see her again," he says.

Little does he know that there's work to be done, and he won't get to see her for who knows how long.

Where will this old man go? They wouldn't send him down to do the reaping, would they?

"My dad died about a year ago. Cancer," I say, but I'm not sure why.

Where are you, Dad? Are you in paradise? Enjoying the sun and eating gourmet dinners with people you lost when you were younger?

He's the first to come to mind when death is mentioned.

Martin nods like he knows. "Cancer takes the best of them, doesn't it," he says. All the sudden I want to cry.

For Martin.

For Mom.

For myself.

Before I realize it, the tears run down my face. I hadn't wanted to cry, especially not in front of him. But I guess sometimes it just happens.

"I'm sorry. I didn't want this job. I just want to see my dad again. Just like you want to see your daughter." I cry, even though I should be doing my job and taking the soul.

The old man nods again. "I know it. I know it."

He finishes the last of his drink. Then stands up and pats his leg. The dog walks over to his side. She moves slow too.

"Let's get this over with," he says. His voice doesn't sounds scared. He sounds ready. I stand up and walk close to him. Before I touch his shoulder, he interrupts me.

"Just do one thing for me," he says.

"What?" I ask.

"Let Dolly come with me. I don't want her to be here alone. She's been my best friend for almost fifteen years," he says.

I look down at the dog. She's still smiling.

I've never seen a dog smile before. For some reason looking at her gives me a little bit of comfort.

I can do this.

Who knew a dog could smile like that?

Am I allowed to let her go too? Would anyone notice? Where does she go after she dies? Doggy heaven?

Do all dogs go to heaven?

"Okay," I say.

Who cares about the rules, I want him to be happy. I don't want Dolly to be here alone, without her best friend.

"Thank you," Martin says. He leans down and pets Dolly. She lets out a whine, but it sounds like a happy one. Martin sets his cup down and then puts a leash on Dolly.

I follow him out to the front yard. He walks to the middle of the weeds.

"I'm ready when you are," he says to me.

The sun is about to go down and the weather is hot. There's a slight breeze that smells like the last bits of summer. I walk close to Martin.

"I'll see you on the other side," he says to me. I touch him on the shoulder.

No burst of light comes from me. I don't see his soul escape his body.

But I do feel pain. A shock to my heart. It's so sudden, that I almost fall over. My head starts to pound.

Martin doesn't look like he's felt a bit of pain.

But he does looks different. Lighter. Happier. Like a weight has been lifted off his shoulders.

Before I can talk myself out of it, I lean down and pet Dolly on her doggy shoulder. She makes a little grunting noise. And then licks my hand.

"Thank you," Martin says. He picks up Dolly and cradles her like she's a puppy.

My head pounds harder.

I turn from them and run away.

I hope my work here is done.

21

Buster

"He's dead, Rosie! He died," Carrie said. She was crying on the phone.

Buster. Her cat.

He'd eaten a whole bag of rice the night before. Mom thought it was kind of funny. I tried my hardest to find no humor in the situation. At least for Carrie. When I told Dad, he gave me a funny look and said, "What a waste of rice."

I'd never heard Carrie so upset. Even though she hated that cat. Always complained to her mom to get rid of him.

"Oh no, really?" I asked. I was only twelve at the time. I'd never known anything or anyone to die. At least no one close to me. This was before Dad was sick.

I sat on my bed and flipped through a magazine, listening to Carrie cry.

"Yes, the vet said his belly just couldn't handle all that rice." She sniffed loud in the phone. Then followed her sniff with a large sob.

I felt bad for the cat. What a bad way to go. With a belly full of uncooked rice. For some reason the thought of something dead made me a little bit sick.

Why was Carrie so upset when she hated the cat?

Maybe I could make her feel better.

"Do you want to have a little kitty funeral for him?" I got off my bed and opened my closet. I had some fancy-looking shoe boxes in there. Maybe we could bury Buster in one of those?

"Mom let the vet keep the body. All I got was his collar," she said.

Relief rushed over me. I didn't have to see the body.

Even if it was just a cat, a dead body was a dead body.

Buster wore a sky blue collar with a little bell on it. That bell annoyed me most of the time, but the thought of never seeing him run around in that collar kind of made me sad.

"We could burn the collar," I said. I'd seen a movie once where a girl burned all her Barbies after she got her first period.

I know it wasn't the same, but maybe it would honor Buster in a way. Plus, we'd get to light something on fire. And that was always fun.

"That's a good idea. I'll have Mom drop me off in a few minutes. Thanks, Rosie," Carrie said.

"Can we burn this in your backyard, Mr. Wolfe?" Carrie said to Dad.

He was in the kitchen cooking dinner. Carrie held the collar out. That annoying bell rang with every step she took.

I could tell Dad wanted to laugh. But he didn't.

He was polite.

He stood at the stove and mashed potatoes.

"Only in the fire pit. But be careful because if that gets out of hand, I'll have to come out with the hose. I do not want to have to do that," Dad said. He used a playful tone. He looked at me and smiled.

"Do you wanna help us, Dad?" I asked.

Dad and I had built the fire pit the summer before. Sometimes we cooked marshmallows over it, and some nights we just sat by it and looked up at the stars.

I loved spending time with him. Even though I was almost thirteen, and most girls my age were embarrassed of their fathers, I wasn't. Carrie thought it was weird, but I didn't care.

"Nah, Rosie, you can do it on your own," he said. Then he held up the potato masher. "Gotta finish these taters."

I lead the way to the back of our yard where we had our little fire pit. Carrie followed, sniffling every few moments.

It was kind of cold outside. A chilly spring breeze came through and gave me a shiver. At least the yard was starting to turn green again.

The flowers were coming back and the grass was getting soft.

It was a good night for a cat funeral.

We got the fire started and stood around the pit. Carrie brought a small iHome player to have soft background music.

"Do you want to say a couple words?" I asked, looking down at the fire. The sun was about to set. I was wrapped in a small blanket with Carrie. She held the collar and stared at it.

She looked so sad.

Sadder than I'd ever seen her.

"I just want to say that . . . Buster, even though you were the most annoying cat in the world, I still loved you." She started to cry again.

The music in the background was some corny pop song that Carrie and I had been obsessing over for the last few weeks. It played on repeat.

"I'm sorry that you ate all that rice. I wish it hadn't been left out on the floor. And even though your litter box was disgusting, I'll even miss cleaning that out for you," she said.

Carrie made a big sigh and then looked at me. "It's your turn, Rosie. Say something about Buster, and then I'll throw the collar in."

I thought about it for a minute.

Buster the cat.

He was overweight and had fluffy orange hair. I'm terribly allergic to cats, so I tried to stay away from him most of the time.

He would cry when he didn't get food. I'd never seen a cat cry until I met Buster.

"Okay. Uh, Buster, you were such a nice, sunny shade of orange. Everyone thought you were super cuddly and sweet. You will be missed," I said. I looked at Carrie. She did another dramatic sigh and then threw the collar in the pit.

"He's gone," she said.

Carrie sat down by the fire and stared at it. I sat next to her. It was nice feeling the heat come off the flames.

"Rosie? Can I tell you something without you thinking I'm a terrible person?" She looked at me. Her mascara was smeared down her face, and most of her lipstick was worn off.

"Of course," I said.

Carrie paused for a minute and then said, "I hated that cat. I hated him. And I'm glad he's gone."

The next thing I knew we were both laughing our faces off.

"I didn't like him much either," I said.

Carrie laughed harder than I'd ever seen her laugh.

When she finally calmed down, she put her arm around my shoulder. "Thanks for being here for me. Even though Buster kind of sucked, I'm glad we did something for him."

It was the first funeral I'd ever been to. And it ended in laughter and hugs.

I was glad about that.

22

Dead Girl

"You did it. The first one is always the hardest," Martha says. She stands by the front door and waits for me.

I feel so exhausted I want to fall into a bed and sleep for the next year. Martha hands me a warm cup of cider.

"Drink that. It'll help with the pain."

I follow her into her living room where she has three couches covered in pillows and blankets. They look expensive. The pillows are soft and silky.

The cider tastes great, and already I feel a tiny bit better. I sit on the couch across from Martha and bundle up.

My whole body shakes.

"They didn't warn me about the sick feeling," I say. "What happened out there? It felt like he took a part of me with him."

Or something.

As light and happy as Martin looked, I feel the exact opposite.

Martha stretches her big body out on the couch. She grunts, like she's been at work all day.

Maybe helping me collect souls is exhausting, but not as exhausting as collecting the soul yourself.

The living room is cozy and warm. The walls are a buttery yellow and the carpet is pale pink.

Flavorful colors.

Colors Mom would love.

Even though it's hot out, chills run throughout my body.

"Everyone experiences something different. Some Reapers have relief, others feel depressed. It depends on the person," Martha says. "But look at the bright side: Just two more souls to go and you can leave. It'll be a little while before you get your next name. Just relax," Martha says. She closes her eyes, like she's going to take a nap.

"I'm just supposed to sit here for the rest of the day and maybe tomorrow and do nothing?" I say. The feeling that soul gave me has made me antsy, angry, and confused.

Martha opens her eyes and turns to me. She gives me an annoyed look. "I'm here to help, not entertain. Go for a walk, or cook some dinner, I don't care. I'm gonna take a nap." Martha turns from me and closes her eyes. Then she puts a pillow over her head, something Mom used to do when she was exhausted.

I drink the rest of the cider and go up to my room. I change into a fresh T-shirt and some dark shorts. Every time I look at myself in the mirror I'm surprised. One thing I will never miss is the acne. Being dead has some perks.

The shakes start to leave, and my brain feels normal again. I'm glad that the cold only lasted a few minutes; otherwise, I don't know if I could take the last two souls.

I glance at my phone to see if Brandy called or messaged me. Nothing.

Just a screen with space and stars in the background.

Should I call and let her know that I collected the first soul?

No. I don't think that's part of the job. At least not my job.

I pull the phone back out and dial Mom's number. It takes a minute before a recorded voice answers.

"The number you have reached is not in service." The recording hangs up on me and all I hear is a dial tone.

We've had the same number for years. Mom would never change it, unless something happened to her.

It's only been a few days since I died, so why is the phone disconnected? Did something happen? Something besides my death?

I dial the number again and hear that same recording. I double-check the phone number. Then triple-check it.

Is it this phone?

I go downstairs to talk to Martha. She's on the couch, snoring. I decide not to wake her and go back outside.

The sun is almost all the way set, and the air has cooled down a lot since this afternoon. I sit on the steps outside of the house and look at the phone again.

The contacts list only has Brandy in it. I can't call her and ask why Mom's phone number is disconnected. Could I even send a text to someone from this phone?

I don't know why, but I start to worry.

Why isn't Mom picking up?

Why is her phone disconnected?

If she was hurt, wouldn't I have known?

"Rosie, what's up?" I look up from the phone and see Kyle. He crosses the street and heads in my direction. He wears a white V-neck. It shows his tan chest. It looks soft. I try not to stare at him.

"Hello." I put the phone in my pocket. Act cool. I can act cool.

He gives me one of his gorgeous smiles that make me grin from ear to ear. I probably look like a freak.

"You gonna come visit me and Penny?" he asks. I'd forgotten he wanted me to play catch with him and his little sister.

Martha said it was a terrible idea, but maybe it would clear my head.

I've never hung out with a guy as cute as Kyle, or any boy for that matter. That was Carrie's thing. I just sat in the background or tagged along.

The third wheel.

"I could maybe come over for a little bit. I have to be back soon though, before Martha wakes up from her nap."

"Great!" Kyle says. He holds out his hand to pull me up. I look at it for a second. Will I make him sick?

Am I going to feel that spark again? Why did that happen?

I reach up and grab his hand.

Nothing happens.

Even though I'm a dead girl, I'm glad someone wants me around.

23

Gone

We walk toward Kyle's house. A few blocks down I see an
ambulance and a couple police cars.

Martin? Did it work?

His soul must be officially gone. He's dead.

"What's going on?" I ask, pointing to the fire truck. Even
though I know what's going on.

I'm the reason it's happening.

"Our neighbor just dropped dead about an hour ago," Kyle
says. He doesn't really sound too sad about it.

Maybe he knew Martin was miserable being alive without his
daughter.

"How did that happen?" I say. I try to sound confused, and
surprised, but I'm not sure if I'm very convincing.

"A stroke or something. But the weird part is, his old dog that he walked around all the time with, she died too," Kyle says.

Dolly.

I'm glad he didn't leave her behind. Now I just wish I knew where she went.

"That's sad," I say.

It is sad. Even though he wanted to go, for some reason my heart feels a stab of guilt.

Did I take his life? Or set him free?

I guess I won't know until I go back.

Or maybe I'll never know.

Kyle shrugs. "Mom thinks it's for the best. She said that after his daughter died he was a depressed old man." Kyle leads me into his yard and then to the front door.

When he lets me in, I am reminded of family.

What it's like to have one.

His brother sits in the living room and plays some video game on the TV. He shouts at the screen.

A woman, probably his mom, hollers from the kitchen for him to shut up. And right when Kyle walks in, Penny runs to him.

"You're home!" She wraps her little arms around him in a hug.

It makes me miss my family.

"Penny, do you remember Rosie? She's here to visit us. Say hello," he says.

Penny stands in front of me now. Brave, unlike this morning. When she was too scared to say hi.

"I'm Penny. Have you ever gone roller-skating?" She has a high, squeaky voice. It makes me want to laugh. She wears a light purple tank top and cutoff jean shorts. Her hair is pulled back into two little pigtails.

She looks adorable.

"Mom bought me pink skates for my fourth birthday. Do you wanna see them?" she says. Her squeaky voice sounds excited when she speaks.

"Penny, don't pester Kyle's guest," a woman shouts from the kitchen.

"I'm not, Mom. She's here to see me. Huh?" Penny looks up at me. She has dark eyes like Kyle.

She walks toward the kitchen and then waves me over.

The three of us follow Penny into the kitchen, where a tall woman with long brown hair stirs something on a skillet.

"Hi, I'm Carolina. You're the girl visiting Martha?"

The food smells like home. The sink is full of dishes and the table has stacks of books on it.

It's nothing like Martha's house, but somehow it's still cozy.

"Yeah, I'm just gonna be here for a few weeks," I say. At least I think I'll be here only a few weeks. Less, if I'm lucky.

"Well, I'm surprised to meet you. Most of Martha's guests are in and out of that place within the week. Half the time we don't even notice them leave."

They shouldn't have noticed me.

I'm not as good of a Reaper as the others, I guess.

"It's true, her guests come and go so often we don't even pay attention anymore," Kyle says.

"She has us working most of the time. But luckily she wanted to take a break," I say.

The feeling in this kitchen makes me homesick. I can feel the love Carolina has for her kids.

I miss feeling that love.

Mom.

I can't stop wondering why her number was disconnected

when I called. Now more than ever I want to call her. Just to hear her voice. To find out if she's okay.

"What are you guys going to do? We have a garage that needs to be cleaned out, why don't you do that?" Carolina says, looking at Kyle.

He laughs and then shakes his head.

"No way. I'll clean it tomorrow. We were gonna play catch outside, and Penny was gonna show Rosie her mad skating skills."

"Yeah! I wanna show Rosie my tricks," Penny says.

Carolina laughs and then looks at me. "You'll have to excuse Penny's excitement. Kyle doesn't usually bring pretty girls around."

"Or girls in general," Mitch shouts from the living room.

Everyone in the kitchen laughs.

"Come on," Penny says. She grabs my hand and pulls me outside with her. Kyle follows us.

Penny runs to a pair of skates and holds them up for me to see.

"Here are my skates. Do you wanna see me do some tricks?" I can't help but grin every time I hear her squeaky voice.

Hanging out with her and Kyle makes my heart ache.

Thoughts of Mom won't leave my head. No matter how much I try to distract myself.

Is she alone? Does she have someone there to comfort her?

I have to try calling her again.

I have to contact her. No matter what the consequences are.

24

Kyle

"Penny likes you," Kyle says. We both walk to Martha's house.

The air is cool out and the moon is high in the sky. There isn't a cloud up there, and the moon lights the street like a midnight sunset.

"She's really sweet. Your whole family is sweet. That was nice of your mom to let me eat with you guys," I say.

Carolina had insisted that I eat family dinner with them. She cooked a Thai stir-fry. It wasn't as good as Dad's. But it was nice being around a family.

People who are alive. And who love one another.

"You probably get homesick while you're away. Please eat with us. A good home-cooked meal," she had said.

Mom.

I wish I knew how she was doing. I worry about her worse than Dad. She's all alone.

I keep pushing the thoughts out of my head, but they keep coming back.

"My whole family likes you," Kyle says. Then he stops walking for a minute and grabs my hand.

This time I feel the spark in my stomach. Butterflies?

Maybe it's because I've never held a boy's hand before.

His skin is soft and warm. I'm probably blushing, but it's so dark out here, I hope he can't tell.

"I like you too, Rosie," he says. He gives me one of those gorgeous smiles.

My face burns after he says this.

How can he like me?

"You don't even know me," I say, looking away from him. If he knew that I was the reason that old man died, I bet he wouldn't like me.

If he knew that I was just a dead girl, doing my work so I can move on to the next life, he probably wouldn't hold my hand.

A Reaper.

Not very cute then.

"I know that you're sweet, and my little sister likes you. She's a great judge of character," he says. We start walking again. "And I know that I'd like to get to know you better."

He holds my hand tight as we walk.

I jerk my hand away, remembering what Charles said about touching the living. What if he gets sick? What if he dies? I don't want him to die.

"You okay?" he says. I'm worried I embarrassed him.

I quickly cough into my hand. I don't know if it sounds forced to Kyle or not.

"Sorry, I think I have allergies," I say. Horrible excuse. But I don't care. It's better than him getting hurt because of me.

He laughs, but doesn't take my hand again. I'm relieved, but also disappointed.

Is this what it feels like to have a boyfriend?

I'd like to get to know him better too. But I know that isn't possible. I've already broken the rules spending the time I've spent with him.

Does Brandy know I held Kyle's hand?

Does she even have time to check up on me?

I pull my phone out of my back pocket and check my messages.

Nothing.

"I wish I could hang out with you again, but I don't think I'm going to have time."

I don't want to say it. It kills me to say it, but I have to. I don't want to get caught. The rules were not to be taken as a joke. And if I mess up, Martha told me they would send me harder souls to take.

"Oh," Kyle says. He sounds hurt, and for some reason when he says this, it shoots pain through my heart.

Is that normal?

Why does something so small make my heart feel so alone?

"I understand," he says. We come up on Martha's house. It's lit up, as usual, with every light on.

"Maybe I could try to visit tomorrow. I just don't know what she will have me doing," I say, gesturing to the house. I shouldn't say it. I know it's not allowed. But maybe Brandy won't find out.

"Really?" Kyle says.

In the back of my mind, I tell myself that I'm making a mistake. Maybe I'm overreacting though? I haven't gotten complete control of this new body and mind and I'm just worrying about nothing.

At the same time, I still have a bad feeling about it. But I nod anyway.

"I'll try to stop by. Will you be home around this same time tomorrow?" I ask. It's about nine o'clock at night. I wonder if Martha is awake. She has to be awake. It's been hours since I left.

"Of course," Kyle says.

I don't understand why he wants to see me so much. I've never gotten this kind of attention from anyone.

This new face.

This new hair.

This new me.

"It was nice hanging out, Rosie," Kyle says. Before I realize it he's put his arms around me in a hug.

He smells like clean laundry. I breathe him in for a moment, and then put my arms around his neck, careful not to grab or touch his shoulder.

"Maybe I'll see you tomorrow," I say.

I walk into the house and am greeted by a very large, very angry Martha.

"Do you just think that the rules don't apply to you, Rosie Wolfe?" Martha shouts. She slams the door behind me and then storms into the kitchen.

I don't think I've seen this woman happy for more than five minutes.

"Martha, don't yell at me. You told me to go for a walk," I say.

And she had. Just wanted me out of her hair. So I got out of it.

She turns around and raises her hands in the air. "Do all your walks consist of hugging the neighbor boys? No, the *living* neighbor boys!" she shouts.

"What? Are there dead neighbor boys I could be hugging? What do you expect? I'm out here all alone. I can't talk to my family. Who knows where my mom is. I've never done this before, Martha," I shout back. Then I turn from her and head upstairs to my room. She follows me.

"Rosie. This isn't a joke. This is your future, your life, and I promise, you're going to regret it. You may be able to hide this from Brandy, and Miss Queen Reaper, but when all this is said and done, you won't like the outcome of that friendship," Martha says. "You'll leave him sooner or later. Sooner is always better."

I ignore her and keep walking. Then go into my room and slam my door.

It's like a fight with a stranger. A stranger you have to live with.

25

Hot

"Bradley wants to take me out," Carrie said. We both sat out on her front porch.

It was hot. Summer hot.

We'd been out of school only a few weeks, and already Carrie was getting asked out on dates.

I, however, was sitting around, waiting for my father to die.

"What did he say?" I had a bag of Doritos next to me and a thirty-two-ounce Big Gulp from 7-Eleven. I was on a junk food binge, and didn't even care that my skin got worse every day.

I was raised where food made me feel better, with Dad's cooking, and Mom's baking. There was always a treat or two around.

Until now. Dad was too sick to cook, and Mom was too depressed to bake.

So I got my fill on Slurpees and candy. Junk food I could just buy at any gas station.

"He messaged me on Snapchat and asked if I liked movies. What girl doesn't like movies?" Carrie said. She grabbed my Coke and took a sip, then continued talking.

"I hear that movies are bad places for first dates, but maybe he will at least hold my hand. Do you think he'll try to kiss me?" Carrie said. She looked at her nails. They were painted bright yellow.

I glanced at my nails. They were all chewed off. I used to paint mine pretty colors like hers, but I stopped worrying about it.

"I'd bet he will. You're a lot better-looking than he is," I said.

Bradley was a junior at our school. He wore expensive-looking clothes and had his hair cut short. He played football, and he wasn't nice to a lot of my classmates.

But he was popular, and I think that's why Carrie liked him.

"Oh, you're too nice to me, Rose Bud," Carrie said.

She called me Rose Bud a lot back in those days. I didn't care for it, but I never complained about it either. There was no point.

"Maybe he has a friend who could take you," Carrie said.

"I doubt that," I said, eating another Dorito. Cool Ranch. My favorite flavor. I wished I had some hot sauce to dip the chips in.

"What about Eric Rogers?" Carrie looked at me with a grin on her face.

Eric Rogers was the fattest boy in our school. He rarely wore deodorant and was one of the kids Bradley would make fun of.

Once, I saw him picking fries off the lunchroom floor and eating them. It made me sick.

"Set it up," I said. I didn't feel like playing this game with Carrie. Boys liked her. She was pretty and had nice clothes.

Boys didn't even look my way. I didn't have time to care about it. All I worried about was Dad getting better.

"You know I'm just playing. Lighten up a little bit." Carrie pushed my shoulder. "Let's go find me something to wear." She stood up and dusted off the back of her shorts.

I didn't move from where I sat. Just put another Dorito into my mouth and washed it down with Coke.

"Are you coming?"

I shrugged. I didn't feel like looking at makeup and tiny skirts. Or talking about boys. I wanted to talk about myself.

I wanted to talk about Dad. And what I was going to do when he was gone for good, and how I was going to handle the sadness.

"I'll stay here," I said.

The sun burned down on the top of my head and I didn't even care. It felt nice. I felt sweat under my armpits but pretended not to notice. The boy who lived across the street from Carrie's family rode around on his bike. He was about four. He looked like he was having a great time. I could hear him laughing every few minutes.

"Uh, why?" Carrie said.

I looked up as she folded her arms across her chest. She didn't look happy. She gave me her "snarky" face, as I liked to call it. Where she scrunched her nose up a little bit. It kind of reminded me of a pissed-off baby.

"Because I'm sick of talking about boys. I'm sick of looking at clothes for a toothpick. I'm sick of it. Why can't we talk about my life? How I'm going to survive when Dad dies?" When I said this, my voice started to rise. I stood up and stared Carrie in the face.

She wasn't snarking at me anymore. She just looked like she felt sorry for me.

Like I was pathetic. Because I was.

Before I knew it, I was crying. Something I didn't enjoy doing in front of people. But I couldn't help it.

"He's going to die, Carrie. And all you want to talk about is clothes, and boys, and lipstick. How come you don't ask me how I'm doing? Or how he's doing?" I said. The tears rolled down my face, but I lowered my voice. I hadn't meant to shout at her.

She was still my best friend. Even when she talked about stupid stuff.

Normal stuff.

Carrie did a big sigh. Then put her arms around my neck.

"My mom told me not to talk about it, Rosie. I'm sorry," she said into my neck. I'm sure she could feel how much I had been sweating. I probably smelled bad too. But she didn't mention it. She just held me like a best friend should.

"I'm sorry about your dad," she said. And I could tell that she was crying too.

Did she also worry Dad was going to die? Had her mom talked to her about it?

Carrie had known my family for years. Since we were babies.

She'd slept at my house hundreds of times, and almost every morning after those sleepovers, Dad cooked us breakfast.

"What are we going to do?" I asked. Carrie smelled like candy. Even on this sweaty summer day, she smelled nice.

"I'll be here for you."

26

Brandy

I wake up to my cell phone ringing. At first I'm not sure what it is. The sound is a bird chirping.

I stumble around in the dark, trying to find where I left the phone.

Then I see the glow of it underneath my sock, right by the window. I grab it.

"Hello?" My voice comes out hoarse. What time is it? It has to be well after midnight.

"Rosie, it's Brandy. I'm just checking up. How are you doing?" she says. She sounds relaxed. Refreshed.

"Well, I was asleep, but other than that I'm fine," I say. Then I yawn into the phone so she knows she woke me up.

Is she calling because of Kyle? Is this a trick? Should I confess my sins and maybe then I won't get into trouble?

"Oh, sorry. The time difference is a killer. I didn't realize. I just got to work and guess what was sitting on my desk?" she says. I imagine her at her desk, typing on her magical computer. Drinking coffee.

"I don't know?" I say.

Is it a report? A report of me being at Kyle's house? Of him holding my hand? What will she say?

Maybe I should just confess.

No. Stay cool. She doesn't know anything.

If I confess they might have my next soul be a four-year-old boy and his puppy. I wouldn't like that at all.

"Martin Gables's file. You got your first soul. That was much faster than a lot of our other Reapers. Congrats," Brandy says.

Relief floods all over me. I'm in the clear.

"There is one tiny little problem though, Rosie, and that's why I'm calling," Brandy says. All of a sudden her tone sounds angry.

Or am I overworrying?

I walk over and flick on the light to my bedroom. Then I sit down on the floor.

Just relax.

Breathe.

No need for panic. Yet.

"What's the problem?" I ask, trying to sound innocent. Even though I'm not. I've held the hand of the living. Martin knew I was a Reaper. What if they add six more souls for me to send back? They can't do that. It's not in the contract, is it? Maybe I should have read it.

"Well, the file says you took the dog as well. Dolly the dog. Is this true?" Brandy says.

Shoot. I had forgotten all about the dog.

Martin and his best friend. I couldn't leave the dog alone in this world.

"I did. He asked me to." The second the words come out of my mouth I want to reach into the phone and take them back.

Nononono!

"Excuse me?" Brandy says. This time I know her voice is angry.

"I didn't mean that. It's just, the dog was so old," I say, stumbling around on my words. Not sure how to get out of this one.

Good-bye, Dad. I'll never see you again.

This time for good.

"He found you out?" Brandy says. Now she whispers into the phone. It sounds like a snake hissing on the other end. I bet if she came back to earth she would come back as a python. Just so she could bite my face off.

"It wasn't my fault. I knocked on the door, and he already knew. I don't know how, Brandy. I never once told him, I swear," I say.

I think about Martin, and his poor old dog. And how sad he was that his daughter was dead. He wanted to go. He wanted to be with his family again.

"How could you let this happen, Rosie? Do you realize what kind of trouble you could get into if someone up here found out?" Brandy says.

Yes. She would come back as a snake. A snake with gorgeous curly hair. And she wouldn't care about collecting souls. Only collecting me.

"I know, I'm sorry, I promise, it won't happen again," I say. "I don't know how he knew what I was, Brandy. He just did, and he asked me to let the dog go too. I promise. I didn't tell him anything else."

Brandy does a big sigh on the other end of the phone.

"All right. This kind of thing happens from time to time, just, don't tell anyone. I'm going to take care of the dog situation up here. But next time, Rosie, don't take the pets. Someone else has that job," she says. Her tone has softened. Which makes me relax a little bit.

"I won't. I promise," I say, relieved. I thought that was it. I thought I was never going to see Dad again.

"Listen. I'm not going to count this as a strike. But if something like that happens again, there will be consequences. Understood?"

Would holding Kyle's hand count as a strike?

At least he doesn't know I'm dead.

"Understood," I say.

"Great!" Brandy uses her cheery tone again. The snake in her is gone. "I'll send you your next soul in a few hours. Go back to bed, and never speak of this again. Pretend like I didn't call. Thanks," Brandy says, and then hangs up the phone.

My heart races, but I feel okay.

I crawl back into bed.

Everything's fine.

27

Mail

"**Get up.** Your second name arrived this morning. The sooner the better, Rosie."

I open my eyes to see Martha standing in the doorway to my room. She wears her apron again. I smell waffles coming from downstairs.

"How?" I sit up and rub my eyes. I look at the cell phone.

No messages. No nothing.

That's when I remember the phone call from last night. Almost like it was a bad dream.

The sun comes through the window and brightens up my room.

Today will be a good day. I have a feeling.

"It came in the mail. Hurry, the food's getting cold," Martha says. Then she closes the door behind her.

At least she doesn't seem mad anymore. Maybe she's used to us Reapers acting out. Being stupid. All I know is I'm relieved. It could have been a lot worse.

The fight with Martha and the phone call with Brandy.

Today will be an easy day.

I can do this. Only two souls away from seeing Dad again.

I brush my teeth and hair and go downstairs to where Martha is. She sits at the counter and smokes a cigarette. I don't know why she does, it ruins the smell of the food. Even though I don't like it, I sit next to her. She already has a plate made for me.

"How'd you sleep?" I ask. Martha has dark circles under her eyes.

She inhales the cigarette, then blows the smoke away from me.

"It was a hard night, Rosie. I fell asleep worrying. About *you*."

I look down at my plate. The smell makes my mouth water. The eggs are fluffy and the waffle looks perfect. It reminds me of Saturday mornings with Dad.

He loved cooking breakfast.

He made all kinds of fun things for me and Carrie when we had sleepovers. Peanut butter and chocolate pancakes. Stuffed French toast.

"I'm sorry, but you shouldn't worry about me," I say. I take a bite of the waffle.

It tastes just as good . . . if not better than Dad's waffles.

This woman can cook. Every bite I take brings back more memories of Dad.

"I want you to make it back, Rosie. I don't want you to be stuck here with me, or at the office, until the end of eternity. Do you realize how long that is?" Martha says.

It's the first time she, or anyone, has talked about what happens after all of this ends.

The world.

Does it?

I don't want to think about it, so I take another bite. Better than the last.

"I'm not going to mess up anymore," I say. And I mean it. I want this to be over just as much as I did on the first day.

But I also can't help thinking about Kyle. How I won't ever see him again after this.

What are a few hours of talking in the whole scheme of things? And Brandy had no idea, so I don't think any red flags have gone up.

I've never met a boy like Kyle.

Sweet.

Cute.

Loves his family.

"I know what you're thinking, Rosie. I was a teenage girl once too. Only I had much easier circumstances. You're making a mistake getting close to that boy." Martha takes another drag of her cigarette. Then she gets up and tosses it in the sink, and rinses off the dishes.

"I'm not thinking anything," I say. Even though my brain has run me back to the night before.

Kyle telling me he likes me.

Holding my hand.

His amazing smile.

Martha looks at me and then smirks. Like she really does know what I'm thinking. I try to hide my smile from her but I can't.

"That's what I thought," she says. Then she tosses me an

envelope. "Second soul. Eat up, and then let's go find them."

The stamp on the envelope is a wildflower. A red wildflower. There's no return address, just my name.

Who sent this?

Brandy? Or Miss Queen Reaper herself?

I open up the letter and read the second name.

> **Name: Cody Bingham**
> **Age: 43**
> **Occupation: pharmacist**
> **Cause of death: cancer**
> **Cody worked as a pharmacist until about two months ago. He has a wife and two young daughters. You must be very careful with a soul like this. There are family members you can't distract. Just a slight touch on the shoulder. Etc.**

I drop the paper on the counter.

No.

I will not.

"No, no way," I say. I feel a lump forming in my throat and my eyes fill with tears. The kitchen all the sudden feels dark and sad. Like I've walked into a storm.

"What is it?" Martha asks. She walks around to where I sit and tries to read the paper.

"Is this some kind of sick joke?" I'm crying now. Fat tears roll down my face. "I won't do that. I can't do it." I shake the paper.

The name.

The cause of death.

Did they plan this?

Are they trying to hurt me?

I'm being punished after all. Just like Martha warned me about.

"I won't," I say to Martha. My voice comes out loud and angry. Then I leave the kitchen and walk out the front door. It slams behind me.

28

Finding Out

"Cancer?" Mom said.

We sat on our couch in the living room. Dad had told us it was time for a family meeting. He made snacks, cleaned up the house, and even dressed in a nice button-up shirt.

I thought it was going to be good news. I thought he was writing another cookbook.

I thought anything but what he told us.

"What do you mean you have cancer? I don't understand," Mom said. She looked like she was going to throw up. Her face had lost all color. She held a little plate with some cheese and crackers on it. She looked almost silly, sitting there holding the plate, with that shocked look on her face.

I'd just taken a bite of cookie when Dad made the announcement. It was like chalk in my mouth now. I grabbed my glass of water and drank it.

"The doctors were suspicious of it when I went in a few months back. It was confirmed this morning. I'm as surprised as you are," Dad said. He used a hopeful tone. Like it wasn't so bad. Like this was just another bump in the road. Like our car breaking down, or an unexpected bill.

"Why are you so relaxed?" I said. I managed to swallow my food without choking. But I still felt like I had a lump in my throat. Maybe it was cancer too. Cancer from holding back tears.

"I have to be relaxed, Rosie. I can beat this. I can," Dad said. He sat down next to Mom and rubbed her back. "It's going to be okay, I promise," Dad said.

But I knew.

I knew. It wasn't going to be okay.

"What stage?" Mom said. She was sniffling now. Not quite crying, but close to it.

"That doesn't matter. What matters is we can beat this. Together we'll be able to beat this," Dad said.

Mom scooted away from him. "Tell me, Josh. Tell me now," she said. Her tone angry and confused.

"We need to know, Dad. How bad is it?" Now I was crying. I could tell by the look on Dad's face that *he* didn't even believe he could beat it.

He looked frightened.

Lost.

Sad.

I'd never seen him look like that.

"It's, uh . . ." Dad cleared his throat. And then looked down at his hands. "It's stage four," he said in a quiet tone.

Mom burst into tears. I stood up and threw my plate on the floor.

"No!" I shouted, and then I walked out of the room.

Cancer.

I imagined it being an evil blob that took over houses and families and ruined their lives. I always pictured it this way.

But then Dad told me he had it. He had that big scary blob inside his body (maybe a cell? I don't know) and it *had* taken over his body.

"Rosie, please," Dad called after me. But he stayed with Mom. I could hear her sobbing, and him saying everything's going to be fine.

Everything's going to be just fine.

But nothing was fine.

And he was going to die.

29

No

I sit on the front porch and cry into my hands. If I had somewhere to run away to, I would. But there's nowhere for me to go.

I'm alone on this earth with no one but myself and my little cell phone that connects me to another world.

How could she do this to me?

Was this Brandy's doing, or was it that evil woman's doing? The true Reaper. The lazy jerk who couldn't just do her own job.

How does she expect me to take the soul of a father?

She must have done it on purpose. She must have found out about Kyle, and decided to punish me to teach me a lesson. Or was it because I took Martin's damn dog?

I pull out the cell phone and dial Mom's number again. I just want to hear her voice. I just want her to tell me that it's going to be okay. That I can get through this.

That same message plays back into my ear.

I hang up the phone and dial her number again.

The same message plays. Over and over.

"Why!" I shout.

Instead of dialing Mom again, I click Brandy's name in the contact list. This might not be an emergency to her, but it sure is for me.

The phone rings for a while before she picks up.

"Rosie, what's the problem?" Brandy sounds like she knew I was going to call. Like she was expecting it.

Of course she knew I was going to call.

"How could you do this to me, Brandy? You knew about my dad. You knew," I say. I cry into the phone and don't even care. I may sound hysterical, may even look hysterical out here by myself crying. But what does it matter? None of it does.

"What are you talking about?" Brandy says. Her voice comes out loud and annoyed.

I take a few breaths.

Be calm.

Just be calm.

"The name, Brandy. The name you sent me this morning. I can't collect a soul like that," I say.

The front door opens behind me and Martha comes out. She holds a pink cupcake on a small plate.

She sits next to me on the porch and hands me the cupcake.

"Eat this, it'll help," she whispers.

The cupcake is beautiful. Like something you would buy at one of those fancy little gourmet bakeries. I shake my head when she holds it out to me.

"Which name are you talking about?" Brandy asks. This time she does sound confused.

Is this an act?

"Cody Bingham, two daughters, dies of cancer. Brandy, I can't do it. Why would you pick that name?" I try to hold back the tears, but when I say "cancer" they spill out again.

Martha sets the plate down next to me, and then rubs my back. She doesn't have to, but does anyway, and somehow it makes me feel a little better.

"Rosie, we warned you about breaking the rules," Brandy says. "But I don't pick the names; I don't even look at the names. I just send them." Brandy sounds like she's telling the truth, but I'm still mad.

Not at her.

Not really at anyone.

Except myself.

"How do you expect me to take a soul like that? Is this because I took Dolly?" I couldn't leave that dog all alone. I was doing the soul a favor.

I imagine the people Upstairs going through names, finding everything with the word "cancer" on it, and slapping my name on it. *Make Rosie take that soul. She knows all about cancer.*

"Could be. It sounds like a punishment. But Rosie, I don't know that for sure. It also just sounds like a random name. A lot of people die of cancer," Brandy says. She tries to sound nice on the other end of the line, but she still has an edge to her voice.

"Can I at least get a new name? Someone else? Anyone else?" I know I sound desperate, but there has to be another way.

"I wish I could help you. But this is how it works. This is a hard job, I know. That's why I opted out. But you can't quit, you have to finish, otherwise you won't be able to move on. I'm sorry. But from now on, follow the rules," Brandy says. Then she hangs up.

"No!" I shout into the phone, but it's too late. She isn't there.

It's just me and Martha.

Martha and me.

"Eat that cupcake, it'll help," Martha says again. Only this time she doesn't whisper. "It won't make the sadness go away, but it'll help. I promise."

I look down at the cupcake. It reminds me of something Dad baked me for my fifth birthday party. The only thing it's missing is the edible glitter he made.

"I should have listened to you. I think I'm being punished," I say.

Martha shrugs. "It might just be a random soul, Rosie. Every Reaper has a soul or two that hits close to home. Now eat that cupcake," Martha says.

My fifth birthday. It was my favorite party I ever had. At that age, was everything easy? Did I worry about anything other than if my friends could come out to play?

"This reminds me of Strawberry Shortcake," I say aloud. More to myself than to Martha.

I remember I wore a Strawberry Shortcake dress to that party. It was the theme. And Dad had perfected those cupcakes. I ate so many I got sick. But since it was my birthday, Mom didn't care.

"It is," Martha says.

I take a bite. It brings me back to the birthday party so many years ago. Mom dolled me up, and Dad made the house perfect with decorations. Carrie had given me a Mermaid Barbie that year.

"Where did you get this recipe?" I ask. The cupcake is better than the one from so many years ago. The flavor of strawberry bursts in my mouth, with the creamy frosting on top.

Everything she cooks is like Dad's, only better.

"Can I tell you a story? It's about a soul very similar to you," Martha says. She lights up a cigarette and waits for me to respond.

I take another bite of the cupcake. She's right, I'm starting to feel a little better.

"Sure," I say.

Martha takes a long drag, and then exhales.

"A while back, I had a Reaper who hated every second of this job. He got his first name, and stayed in bed for two days," Martha says. "I remember it was a young girl. He said she reminded him of his daughter from his life before death."

"How old was his daughter?" I ask.

Martha shrugs. "About your age. Maybe a little younger. Anyway, after the second day, I brought him a chocolate brownie."

Kids come out of their houses to play outside. It's getting hotter every second while we sit out here and talk. The sun feels nice, but at the same time it makes me tired. If I could, I would sit in bed for two days too.

"You know what he said when he took a bite of the brownie, Rosie?" Martha says. She smiles when she tells the story. She looks off into the distance like it's a memory she wants to crawl back into.

"No, what did he say?" I'm not sure how this applies to me, but talking does distract me from that stupid name.

Cody Bingham.

Cancer.

His two daughters.

"He said, 'This is the most disgusting brownie I've ever eaten,' then he laughed in my face," Martha says. She laughs when she tells me this. But I don't think it's all that funny.

"That isn't nice at all. Why are you telling me this?" I take another small bite of the cupcake. Every taste is better than the last.

"Because after he said that, he took me downstairs and showed me how to cook. Told me all of his baking secrets. Wrote down all his favorite recipes from his books he wrote before," Martha says.

That's when I realize what she's saying.

It does make me feel better.

"My dad?" I ask. It makes so much sense now. The food, the story, this cupcake. It's all recipes from his books. The stuff he made me when I was a kid. The stuff he made me when I was sad.

The comfort food.

The happy food.

Martha nods. "I tell you this story because, Rosie, I know it's hard. But your dad did it. He did his job down here, and he moved on. And not only did he move on, he left me with something that I can use on all the Reapers that come to my house. Comfort. Happiness. Even if it's just on a plate, it still helps."

I want to cry again after Martha tells me this.

If Dad could do it, maybe I can too?

"How come you didn't tell me that he stayed here?"

How could he end up in the same house as me? I know that there are thousands all over the world, just like this. But we got sent to the same house. With the same person.

Martha.

"Because it's against the rules. But you needed to hear it. You need to finish your work, and move on, and stay with your father forever," Martha says.

I lean over and put my arms around her. She smells like smoke and cooking. It takes her a minute, but she hugs me back.

"Thank you," I say.

30

Smoking

"**Cody Bingham lives** just a few miles away from here. His doctors sent him home so he could pass away with his family," Martha tells me. We both get in her old rusty Cadillac.

The car has an ashtray full of cigarettes, and the seats are dusty. When she starts the car up, it makes a loud noise. Like it's a struggle just to get the engine to run.

"Sorry. I don't usually drive," Martha says, giving the car a little gas. "Makes my nerves crazy."

She backs out of the driveway fast, and I jump. "Geez," I say, buckling up my seat belt.

I used to love driving. I only had my permit, but sometimes Mom would let me go on special drives by myself, to have some free time with my mind. I loved to roll down the windows and feel the breeze.

It's almost ironic that something I loved killed me.

An accident.

That last night alive is almost a blur now. The rain beating down on me, the white dog . . .

"Keep that seat belt on," Martha says. She drives fast up the road. Probably too fast for a neighborhood like this, but I don't say anything. I don't think there's any reason to.

If we crashed, would I die again?

"Have you met this man?" I ask, trying not to look outside the window. The more turns Martha takes, the lighter my head feels.

"No, but I know someone who knows someone who works for him. That's how you're going to get inside the house. And that's why I made the cake," Martha says.

I glance in the backseat and see the cake she made. It smells amazing, and it's frosted with a creamy cherry icing.

"This is going to be hard," I say.

I've prepared myself for this for the last three hours. Listening to the stories about Dad that Martha thought would help. I've tried to convince myself it's okay. It'll be easy.

Don't think about the sad stuff.

Cancer.

His family.

His daughters.

I can't think about how I know they don't want him to go. Because I know how they feel, and I never wanted Dad to leave.

"Rosie, you have to remember the pain he's in. And also you must consider your own father. He's waiting for you," Martha says. Then she honks the horn and yells out her window, "What in the world are you doing? Just drive the car, it's not that hard!" When she's done yelling, she looks at me and smiles.

"You're a good driver," I say, trying not to laugh. At least Martha keeps me distracted. I've never met anyone like her.

"Don't be sarcastic, Rosie. It's rude," she says. Then laughs. "Anyway, just get in there, get out, and you're done. I'll be waiting outside in the car." Martha slows the car down and pulls in front of a light blue house. It has two cars in the driveway, and a small bike on the grass in the front yard.

"Is this it?"

From the outside this doesn't look like the kind of place that would hold so much sadness on the inside. It looks like a regular family home. The grass is nice and green with beautiful roses by the front windows. Like someone's taken great care of the yard.

I bet our house looked like a normal house too.

"Yup. This is the place. Do you remember what you're going to say?" Martha says, parking the car across the street from the house. She lights up a cigarette.

I'm supposed to knock on the door and pretend I'm someone who worked in Cody's building. Offer the cake, and then ask to see him.

It sounds simple.

Maybe it will be.

"Yeah, I remember." I watch Martha inhale and exhale the smoke. I've never thought about trying to smoke until now.

"Could I have one of those?" I point to her pack of cigarettes. American Spirits.

Martha flicks ash out the window. "You're not old enough to smoke, Rosie. Plus, they're bad for you."

"What does it matter? I'm dead anyway. Just one. Please?" At this point I'll do anything to calm my nerves.

Martha does a big sigh, and then hands me a cigarette and

lighter. "If you decide to light this, you're finishing it. These are expensive, and I don't want it wasted," Martha says.

I nod. Then put the cigarette in my mouth.

Once, in middle school, Carrie stole a whole pack of smokes from her dad.

"Let's smoke these under the bleachers," she said. A boy named Damon Martin, she, and I all met under the bleachers after school. It was winter then, so it was colder than ever.

Carrie passed each of us a cigarette and held up a box of matches she'd found in the science lab.

"Who wants to go first?"

I looked at her and shrugged.

"What about you, Damon?" she asked.

He waited a minute, and then nodded. "I'll try. My grandma smokes all the time."

Carrie struck the match, and then lit his cig for him.

Before he could exhale, he was coughing his face off.

"Are you all right?" I asked. Right when I said that one of our PE teachers caught us.

I was grounded for a month when my parents found out, even after I told them that I didn't smoke.

I'd never thought of trying a cigarette again after that.

Until now.

I light up the end and inhale. The second I do, I cough, just like Damon had so many years ago.

"Told you," Martha says. She laughs and pats my back. "You're not cut out for those. They're bad for you."

I wait a second to catch my breath, and then try another puff. This time, it's not as bad. But the taste in my mouth is ashy and gross.

"How is this supposed to relieve stress?" I ask, taking another puff. Martha shrugs.

"Just depends on the person, I guess." Then she leans over and takes the cigarette out of my mouth. "I changed my mind. You can't have all this. No more killing time. You need to go in there, collect Cody's soul, and get it over with."

Martha's right. But I still don't want to.

The house looks sadder and sadder every minute. Just because I know what's going to happen.

I know how their story ends.

Finally I get out of the car and walk toward the house. Dreading every last step.

31

Cody

I feel like since I've died and ended up back on earth, I've stood at a lot of doors waiting to knock.

This is by far the scariest door I've seen.

I can hear voices on the inside. I want to peek through the windows, just to see the children so I know what to expect, but I don't. Instead I hold the cake with one hand and ring the doorbell with the other.

It takes a minute, but the door opens just enough for a little girl to stick her head out.

She looks about four years old. She has long, frizzy blond hair and skinny tan legs and arms.

"Hello," she says. She opens the door enough to step outside. She wears a Tinker Bell dress that has stains on the front. It looks too small for her.

"Hi, I'm here to see your mom and dad. Is either of them home?"

The girl opens the door and then shouts, "Mom! A girl is here with cake for Dad, should I let her in?"

The inside of the house has toys strewn about. It smells like something inside may have burned. Maybe toast or popcorn. The smell makes the ashy taste in my mouth stronger. I don't know why.

It takes a minute, but then I hear a voice shout back, "Charlotte, let the guest in. I'll be down in a second."

The girl, Charlotte, waves me in.

I hesitate, then follow her into the entryway.

"What kinda cake is that?" She points to the cake.

"I think it's cherry. I didn't bake it, a friend of your father's did." I know it's a little bit of a lie, but what else can I say?

This job requires a lot of lies.

"Can I try the frosting?" she asks.

Her mom still hasn't come to find me. But I can hear people moving around upstairs. Low voices.

"If you don't think your mom will mind," I say.

Charlotte gives me a grin, and then laughs. "She won't care."

I set the cake down and Charlotte sticks her finger in the frosting. Just as she does, a woman comes into the foyer.

"Charlotte, no," she says in a tired voice. This must be Mrs. Bingham. She walks over and grabs the little girl's arm. "You know you can't have sweets until after dinner. Go upstairs and wash your face. Scoot."

Charlotte runs out of the foyer. Her wavy hair bouncing with every step she takes.

The woman, Charlotte's mother, also has frizzy blond hair.

She's thin. Probably too thin. And has dark circles under her eyes.

"Hello, I'm Janet." She holds her thin arm out and I shake her hand.

"Yes. I came to bring this cake, and to say hello." My voice shakes when I speak. If I'm not careful, I'm going to burst into tears right here. The look on her face reminds me of Mom's. During those last few weeks of Dad's life.

"How do you know Cody?" Janet asks. She doesn't take the cake, just stands there, looking at me.

I freeze, trying to remember the lie.

"I've known him for a while," I say quietly.

Janet folds her arms across her chest and looks at me funny. Like she knows I'm a liar.

"How?" she says. "He's very sick and visitors wear on him, so I'd like to get a little bit of an idea of who you are," she says. Her tone isn't mean, just tired.

I look around the foyer for an answer. Why did I think this was going to be easy?

"He was a friend of my mom. They worked together years ago. Cody would stop by and visit," I say, looking down at the cake. "He was nice to me. I was really young when I met him, but he was so kind. I still remember," I say. The lie hangs in the air.

Does she know?

Does she know who I am like Martin did?

"Oh, how did he know your mother? College?" she asks, giving me the answer to the same question I had.

"Yes. I'm sorry to intrude, I really don't mean to. She just said she's heartbroken she couldn't make it," I say. The lie feels wrong. It all feels wrong.

What if someone lied to my mom like this?

Janet looks a little bit more relaxed and takes the cake from me. "Well, this looks amazing. Your mom must be a great cook."

I'm not sure what to say. I know I need to get in and out of here, but I'm stuck. Not sure what to do or where to go.

How can I do this to her?

Or little Charlotte.

"Let's bring this into the kitchen. We can all have a piece, and then you can go up and say your good-bye to Cody," she says.

My good-bye.

She's ready.

She's been waiting.

I follow her into the kitchen where another girl sits at the table, reading a book. She looks a little bit younger than me.

"Courtney, this is . . ." Janet pauses and looks at me.

"Hi, I'm Rosie," I say. The girl at the table looks up at me and stares for a minute, and then gazes back down at her book.

"Courtney, don't be rude. She brought cake. Would you like to eat some with us?" Janet says. She sounds helpless when she talks to Courtney.

"No, I don't want cake. I want everyone to stop coming here and looking at my father, who's about to die. This isn't a damn zoo." Her voice is harsh and mean. She stands up and walks out of the room.

"I'm sorry, I didn't mean it like that," I call after her. She ignores me.

Janet sits down at the table and puts her hands on her face. "I'm sorry, I really am. I have forgotten how to entertain guests," she says.

"No. I'm sorry, I should just leave," I say. Even though I know I can't. If I could, I would have been out of here the second I saw Charlotte.

I have to get this done. Or I'll never see Dad again.

"It's fine. Cody's upstairs. I'll take you. Let's cut him a small piece of that cake first," Janet says. She gets up from her chair, cuts a small slice of cake, and puts it on a plate.

"You just have to understand that he isn't the same as he was before. Brain cancer changes the mind. He may not remember you. If he's awake at all," Janet says. We walk up the stairs. Toys and clothes are strewn about. The house isn't messy, but it isn't clean, either.

She leads me to a room at the end of the hall. The door's closed, and there's a small sign on it that says QUIET.

"Just keep your voice down," Janet says.

I nod.

The room is dark and smells musky. There's a bed with a frail-looking man in it. He looks like he's dead already. But when Janet steps closer, he opens his eyes a little bit and smiles at her.

"Hey, honey, you have a guest." Janet touches his head and pats his hand. "This nice girl brought you a cake, too. Do you think you could stomach some?"

The man doesn't say anything. Just stares up at her. I can tell that he loves to look at her. He keeps his eyes on her the whole time.

"Sorry, Rosie. He won't be able to eat cake, but come on in. Say hello."

I still stand at the door, not sure if I should interrupt her moment with him.

When I walk into the room, I'm hit with a memory of Dad.

Lying in the hospital. All the tubes hooked up to him, he fell asleep and died.

Is this how Cody will pass?

Janet whispers things to him I can't hear.

I shouldn't be here. It's not right that I'm here. In these last moments of life with her husband. But this is the only way.

I step a little closer to the bed. I have to end this. It's my job. Just keep telling myself this.

"This is Rosie. She's the daughter of someone you grew up with. Do you recognize her?" Janet says. She grabs my hand and pulls me next to her.

He doesn't look at me, but he does shake his head.

"Hi, Cody. My mom was Mary. You went to college with her," I say. I step a little closer to him. Janet is on one side of the bed, so I go to the opposite side of her.

"I just wanted to visit and . . ." I pause. I don't want to lie to this man, or his family. It's not supposed to matter, but I still don't feel right about it.

"I'm leaving town pretty soon. And I wanted to come here and say good-bye. I won't be coming back ever again."

Janet pets Cody's hand as I talk. She stares at him like he's the only person on earth. Like I'm not here. Like I'm a ghost, and soon, he will be too.

I want to leave this place. Let her be alone with him. But if I don't do this, what happens to him? Does he get better? Does the cancer leave? Or does he stay in this dream state with his wife waiting and waiting for him to die? What happens to me?

She looks so sad. Like she can't take any more pain.

I step a little closer to Cody's body.

"Maybe I'll see you again someday," I say. Then I lean over

and touch his shoulder. When I do, I'm hit with a feeling of pain all through my body. It knocks me to the ground.

"Oh my goodness, are you okay?" Janet jumps up and runs over to where I am on the floor. "Did you trip? What happened?"

The sick feeling has come back, only this time it's worse. Much worse.

"I don't know, I think I just need to go." I try to catch my breath. Janet holds her hand out to me and pulls me up.

I glance at Cody. His eyes are wide open. And he stares right at me. I step a few feet back.

"Are you sure you're okay?" Janet asks.

I nod.

"Well, thank you for coming. Sorry Cody wasn't very responsive."

Without thinking I point to him. "He looks responsive. Maybe you two can talk," I say.

Janet turns around and sees Cody. His eyes stare straight at me. He doesn't look angry, but just seeing him like that makes me feel worse.

"Honey, are you okay?" Janet runs to the side of his bed.

That's when I leave.

I'm almost to the front door when Courtney stops me on my way out.

"Did you get a good look at him? Did get to stare at my dying father?" She stands with her hands on her hips. Her tone is harsh and it sounds like she wants to scream at me. Her face is angry and hard. Like she hasn't smiled in years. I can see her hands at her sides, balled into fists.

Does she want to hit me?

Is she going to punch me?

"I just wanted to say good-bye," I say. Trying to sound calm, even though my voice shakes. With each step I feel sicker and sicker. This is a much different feeling from when I took Martin.

It's heavier.

"Are you one of his mistresses? What are you, eighteen? You don't even look that old. Did he meet you online, too?" Courtney blocks the front door. If I wanted to, I could probably push her to the side, but I don't.

"What are you talking about?" I say.

"You know what I'm talking about. He's had so many women in and out of here, and you're one of them. Do you think you're going to get money from him?" She takes a few steps toward me. "There isn't any money left. Not a dime. It all went to his treatment, and none of you will get anything. Nothing from him, or my mom," she says.

Mistresses?

What is she talking about?

"I'm not who you think I am," I say.

Who was this man?

What did he do to his family to make her so angry?

"Then who are you? Why are you here?" she says.

I glance around the entryway. It's just the two of us. I'm glad her little sister didn't have to see this. Glad this wasn't my life.

"I'm a friend. My mom sent me here; she couldn't come," I say. I hate lying, but I'm stuck right in the middle of it. "I promise you, I have nothing to do with whatever it is you think I've done. I don't even know your father."

Courtney stands there and stares at me, and then starts to cry.

"I just want him to die already. I hate him, I hate him so

much," she says. Courtney sits on the floor by the front door. She cries into her hands.

I don't know what to do or say.

I feel like I might throw up from the soul, but I also feel terrible for this girl.

"Don't say that," I say. I walk over and sit next to her. It's everything I can do not to run screaming from this house and vomit in the bushes outside, but I breathe in and out, to try to stop it.

"He was an awful person, and now everyone comes here and acts like he was this great guy. And Mom. She's the worst. She's completely forgotten how he treated her. How he treated the family."

I take another deep breath. Martha is waiting out there for me, and I know she's going to wonder what's taking so long. But I can't just leave Courtney this way. Even though I don't know her.

"Listen. He doesn't have that much longer. And maybe these last few hours or days or whatever, you can try to think about the good in him," I say.

It reminds me of the fights I would sometimes get in with my dad. About stupid stuff. Allowance, curfew, friends. I remember how angry I would get at him and Mom.

And then how guilty I felt about it, after he died, when I would think about those times.

"That's easy for you to say. Your dad isn't dying from cancer," she says.

I feel a stab of pain in my heart.

She's right.

"No, he isn't. But he did die from cancer," I say. My voice comes out defensive.

Courtney looks up at me when I say this. She looks like I've slapped her. Like I'm lying to her face.

"Who are you?" she says.

I stand up, and so does she. I open the front door and walk outside. She follows close behind me.

"Hey! Who are you?" she says.

She follows me all the way to Martha's car across the street. I glance inside and see that Martha is asleep.

I turn around and stare Courtney in the face.

"I'm the girl who ends it all," I say, and then I get in the car.

"Drive," I shout. Martha jolts awake.

"All righty then. Two down, one to go," she says. Then she drives away while Courtney shouts in the distance.

32

After

"**What happened back there?**" Martha says.

She drives fast in the opposite direction of Cody's house. My heart races, and the sickness that I feel is getting worse. It's like a migraine mixed with the flu.

"His daughter followed me out. She wanted to know who I was." I roll down the window. I breathe in the fresh air from outside. It clears my head a little, but not much.

"What for? What did you say to her?" Martha swerves past another car. It makes my stomach flip on the inside.

"I don't know! She thought I was his mistress or something," I say. "I guess he wasn't a great person."

All I want to do is crawl into bed, my *real* bed, and fall asleep until this nightmare is over.

"Oh, you got a bad one. Those throw some Reapers off. I'm

sorry to hear that," Martha says. Then she sighs and turns the radio on. I lean over and flick it off.

"I can't. I feel awful right now," I say.

Martha glances at me, then back at the road.

"Did they at least like the cake?"

When she says this, it reminds me of my father. Even at the worst of times, he wanted to know how the food was. The day he told us he had cancer, he wanted to make sure the food tasted perfect.

Even though I feel like total crap, I laugh. Just a small laugh. The sound of my own voice makes my ears ring.

"What's so funny?" Martha says. I can hear in her voice that she's smiling, and that makes me laugh even more.

"All you want to know is how the cake was? My Dad really did teach you, didn't he?"

"Hey, I worked hard on that cake, Rosie." Martha swerves the car again. I try to ignore it.

Someone in the car behind us honks their horn. I roll up my window to try to drown out the sound.

"I'm sure my dad would be proud. Now drive faster, I got to get in bed." I lean my head against the window and close my eyes.

Just breathe.

"I've heard the bad souls can cause quite the headache. Well, we're almost there. What else did his daughter say?" Martha says.

That girl.

So angry and so sad.

If I had felt that way about Dad, I don't know what I would have done. Will she feel guilty when he dies? Relief?

I guess I'll never know. I'm glad I'll never know.

"She just said she wanted her dad dead, and that he was a bad person," I say.

Martha pulls the car up in the driveway.

She hits a rock or something and it makes the car bump. I feel vomit rise in my throat, but manage to keep it down.

"Come inside, let's eat. It'll make you feel better." She gets out of the car and heads inside.

I hang behind for a minute.

Still thinking about Courtney. She hated her father. In just a few hours she won't ever see him again.

At least not in this life.

Did she ever share good times with him? Was she happy when he told the family that he had cancer?

The whole thing throws me off more than collecting the soul.

I realize now that even though I lost my father early, at least he loved me and Mom.

My head still spins when I walk into the kitchen where Martha cooks. It looks like she's making mac and cheese from scratch.

Dad's recipe. Of course.

"How did Dad seem when he was here?" I ask.

Had he gained his weight back? Did the color return to his face? Was he in pain?

"Ahh, Josh. He was great to be around, wasn't he?" Martha says. She throws some cream cheese in a pot with small pieces of chopped-up bacon.

"Your father talked about you and your mom all the time. He missed you guys. He distracted himself by cooking and getting his work done fast. He collected his souls as a human as well."

I think about Dad being in this kitchen. Teaching Martha how to cook. I never let him teach me. He tried all the time, telling me he wasn't going to be around forever. But I didn't believe him.

"How long was he here?" Talking about Dad makes me feel a little better. The headache still hangs around, but at least my stomach doesn't feel as bad.

"Hmm, I think it only took him four days in total. I miss him," Martha says. She turns around and looks at me. Like she's thinking about a time before.

A time with someone she loved.

"I've already been here three days," I say, more to myself than to Martha.

She walks to the fridge and pulls out the cream. Pours a little bit of it into the pot.

"The last soul always takes the longest. They seem to drag out sending it to you. Mostly because they like to go back and check to make sure the others went through properly," Martha says.

"The food smells good," I say, trying to think of something else.

Martha fills a bowlful of the noodles and pours some of the thick cheese sauce on it.

"Tell me if that isn't the best mac and cheese you've ever had."

I take a bite.

It is the best mac and cheese I've ever had.

Sorry, Dad, but she's a better cook.

33

Mom

After lunch, I take a small nap. I dream about Courtney and her family. I dream that she walks in and finds her father dead, and cheers with joy.

When I wake up, I feel sad for her. Sad that her father had to be the way he was, and that she just wanted him out of her life forever.

I go downstairs to find that I'm alone in the house.

Martha left me a note on the kitchen counter telling me she had to take care of other "business" and she will be back later.

I'm getting everything ready for another guest. You only have a few more days here, got to be prepared, she wrote.

I wonder why they couldn't have just sent me down with another Reaper. Someone to talk to. At least then I would have had someone to relate with.

I decide to walk over to Kyle's house.

They can't expect me to wait around for two days all alone. And I like Martha, but I think she's getting sick of me. I bet she wants me to leave. I bet I'm getting on her nerves every single day. And I don't even blame her. I've been a mess since I got here.

Plus, they've already punished me for something. What could be worse than taking a soul similar to Dad's?

When I get to Kyle's, Penny is playing in the front yard. She wears a swimsuit and sits in a small kiddie pool. Kyle's older brother, Mitch, sits in a lawn chair next to her, reading a book.

"Rosie!" she shouts when she sees me. She hops out of the pool and runs over.

"Hi, Penny. Is this new?" I point to the pool. Mitch sees me and waves.

"I just got it. Do you wanna get in?" Penny says. She jumps up and down when she talks. She's pretty hyper and excited.

Sometimes I miss being that young. So alive and happy. Nothing to worry about. Death wasn't something that was thought about often, and you could just enjoy life.

"I don't have a swimsuit." I point to her swimsuit. It's a little red one-piece with white polka dots.

She looks adorable.

"Do you think I'd fit in yours?" Penny laughs like this is the funniest thing in the world. She has a smile just like Kyle's. Contagious.

When she laughs, I can't help but giggle too.

"You're too big. I can ask my mom. Maybe you can borrow hers," Penny says. Then she runs into the house and slams the front door behind her.

I go to where Mitch sits on the chair.

"She really likes you," he says. He looks a lot like Kyle. Only older with darker eyes and skin. The sun beats down on both of us. A dip in that kiddie pool probably wouldn't even be that bad. At least it would cool me off. I can already feel myself start to sweat.

"I like her, too. She's cute," I say.

"She's not the only one who likes you," Mitch says, then laughs. "Kyle's in the house. He'll be glad you're here. He hasn't stopped talking about you since we picked you up that night."

I feel my face flush as Mitch speaks. I'm not sure what to say to this. I'm embarrassed, but also a little bit excited.

It's all so new to me. But in a way I've never felt. In a way that gives me butterflies. Something I've read about, but never felt until now.

"I don't know why," I say. I know that's not something you're supposed to say, but I don't know how to respond to this sort of thing.

I didn't know anything about boys when I was alive.

How could he like me?

"Don't be so dramatic. You're cute, and you're a lot nicer than the girls around here. He likes that. He needs someone like that. Go inside," Mitch says. He uses a playful tone.

I've never met a family like this. So close, and so open.

I walk into the house and Kyle meets me at the front door.

"Penny told me you were here. Hi," Kyle says. Then he puts his arms around me in a hug.

It's what I needed today. After everything that's happened.

Courtney.

Her father's cancer.

The way that soul made me feel.

Just seeing Kyle makes the sick feeling in my stomach disappear.

"I'm surprised you're here so early," Kyle says. He lets go of me, and we walk into the living room and sit on one of the leather couches. The TV is turned off. It makes me realize that Martha doesn't keep a TV in the house.

I haven't watched it for a long time.

"I got off work early. I'll probably have some free time tomorrow, too," I say.

I have a small nagging in the back of my mind. A feeling that won't go away.

Mom.

I can't get her out of my brain, no matter how hard I try to distract myself.

Seeing Courtney's mother made me ache with loneliness for Mom.

I try to push the thoughts out of my head again, but they don't fully leave.

"That's awesome. I got off work early too. I work at the grocery store down the road from here."

I love to watch Kyle talk.

The way his mouth moves, and the tone of his voice. He's so soft spoken. I wish so much that he was with me when I was on earth.

Would he have liked the real me? The Rosie Wolfe who ate junk food and cried over her father's death?

Maybe not.

Who knew dying would make me become someone boys would talk to. Would like.

"I saw Penny's pool. When did she get that?" I can hear

Penny's voice upstairs. She must be talking to her mom.

"We pulled it out of storage this morning. Mom and I decided to clean out the garage," Kyle says.

"Ah, when I was little I loved swimming. She looks so cute in her swimsuit," I say.

Kyle scoots a little closer to me while I talk. It makes my heart jump. Those butterflies again. Such a weird feeling.

"Me too," he says. "So, what do you want to do today? Should we go on a hike? Or watch a movie?" Kyle says.

I guess I didn't think about that. Coming over so early.

What do normal girls do?

I haven't watched TV since I got here, but hiking could be nice. I'm not sure if I should go too far from Martha's house.

"What kind of movies do you have?" I ask.

When I was alive, I obsessed over the serial killer detective-type movies. Mom and I watched those all the time. She would always figure out who the bad guy was at the very beginning.

"We just bought some new ones," Kyle says. He walks over to the entertainment set and opens one of the cabinets.

He takes out three movies and sits back down on the couch next to me.

"These are some of my favorites."

He holds up an old classic. *The Silence of the Lambs.*

"You actually liked that movie? It's older than we are," I say.

"Sure. It's a classic. Have you read the books?"

I nod. I'm surprised anyone our age likes that sort of stuff. Dead bodies, serial killers, cannibals.

"What else did you pick out?"

Kyle holds up another movie. It's another old one. *Finding Nemo.* The cartoon movie about a fish that loses his father. I loved it when I was younger. Not so much now. I haven't seen it since Dad died. It was one of the last movies we watched together. He loved it.

"Your movie choices are all over the place," I say.

"I guess that means no *Nemo*. Okay, well, this one was just released. Did you see it in theaters?"

When Kyle holds up the DVD, I want to scream.

The Black Bird.

The movie I was going to see on opening night with Carrie, just a few days ago.

The night I died.

"How did you get that?" I point to the DVD.

"What do you mean? I bought it. It came out yesterday," Kyle says. He gives me a confused smile.

I stand up and pace around the room. I don't want to have a panic attack around him, but I'm freaking out.

Just breathe.

"Didn't that just come out on Friday?"

Carrie insisted we sit in line and see the movie. She wanted me to wear something nice. "Boys will be there, Rosie. Wear something cute. No more black," she said. So I went home, and I died on the way.

I never got to see the movie.

But that was only a week ago.

Wasn't it?

"Well, they released the Blu-ray on Tuesday. I just bought this yesterday," Kyle says.

I take the movie from Kyle and look at the back. I read through the description.

It's the same movie.

My head starts to spin again and I feel like I'm gonna have a heart attack.

I pull out my cell phone and dial Mom's phone number.

It doesn't even ring, just says the number is disconnected.

That number worked a few days ago.

I called her on my way to Carrie's. I remember.

"Rosie, are you okay?" Kyle asks. He stands up next to me and rubs my back for a second.

"I just don't understand," I say aloud. Why would her number be disconnected after only a few days?

How could this movie be out already?

I turn and look at Kyle. His eyes are so dark. He isn't smiling, though. He looks worried. Worried because of me.

"Could I see your cell phone?" I ask.

My phone doesn't even have a calendar in it. So why would it let me dial out? Why would it connect me to someone here on earth?

"Sure," Kyle says. He pulls his phone out of his pocket. It's a thin phone with a mirrored back.

I've never seen a phone that looks like this before.

I manage to figure out how the keypad works, and I dial Mom's number again.

It takes a minute for it to connect. But when it does I get the same answer.

The number has been disconnected.

I pull the phone away from my ear and look through the apps till I find the calendar.

"You're kinda freaking me out," Kyle says. Then does another nervous laugh. "Are you snooping?"

"No. Give me a second, I just realized something," I say, looking at the date.

I didn't just lose a few days while I was up there training to become a Reaper.

I lost a year.

How is that even possible?

"I think I need to run to Martha's for a bit," I say, trying to keep my voice calm.

Has she known? This whole time? What if something happened to Mom? Why is her phone disconnected? She's been stuck down here, alone, for a year.

"Can I walk you? Do you want to come back later?" Kyle asks. He sounds a little hurt. I guess I can see why. I'm having a mini freak-out right here in his living room.

"Yes, I'll try to come back," I say. I hand him his phone and put my arms around his neck. He smells clean and happy. Like a world that I wish I could live in. Where no one dies.

He puts his arms around me and holds me for a minute.

"I'll be here," he says into my neck. His breath is warm and makes chills run down my arms.

"Thank you," I say.

Then I run out the front door.

34

Road Trip

I walk inside and see that Martha still isn't home.

Before I know it, I'm snooping through all her stuff. Most of the drawers in her kitchen have just regular silverware and cooking supplies.

The living room only has one bookshelf. And it's piled down with old magazines and soft paperbacks that look a hundred years old.

I'm not even sure what I'm looking for.

If it's been a year, a lot must have changed.

What if Mom moved far away? Remarried? Found a new life? Died?

I start to panic.

What if something *did* happen to her? There has to be a way to find out.

After I died, the only people she had left were her dad and her sisters. She rarely saw them before. Would she go to them now? After she lost her whole family to Death?

To the Reapers?

To things like me.

After a few minutes of looking, I find a newspaper under the couch cushion that Martha always naps on.

So she was hiding it from me.

I pull it out and find the date. It says it's the same day as Kyle's phone said.

How did I lose so much time up there?

I sit on the floor and read through the news. People are dying all over, as usual.

I glance through the classifieds. Pets. Housing. Places hiring. And that's when I notice. This is the paper for the city just a few hours from Mom's house.

From where I grew up. And then died.

When I look closer at the classifieds, I see the area codes. One is the same for our city.

For the city I grew up in.

How can this be? How can I be this close to Mom and not even know it until now? And Martha never even told me.

Did she know?

Did Dad know when he was here?

I take the newspaper with me and go upstairs to my room. There, I inspect it further. I even recognize some of the names in here. Town officials. The college that's been mentioned more than once.

Now I know I have to make sure she's okay.

I have to find Mom.

* * *

"Could you drive me somewhere?" I say to Kyle when he opens the front door.

He gives me another confused look. He probably thinks I'm a weirdo and regrets ever getting to know me. But right now, I don't even care. I want to find my mother. Before the last soul is sent to me. Before I have to leave earth forever.

"Sure. Is everything okay?" He's asked me more than once today. And I don't know how to answer.

I don't want to lie to him anymore, but I know I can't tell him.

"I'm fine, I just, there's somewhere I need to go," I say.

"Okay, you can tell me about it in the car," Kyle says. Then he runs into the house to get the keys to his brother's Subaru. The one they picked me up in the first time I met him.

It feels like so long ago, even though it's only been a couple days.

I get into the car and wait for Kyle. The floor is a lot cleaner this time. Not as many food wrappers or Big Gulp cups.

"Did you clean?" I ask Kyle when he gets in. He gives me one of those smiles and then nods.

"Mom was pissed when she saw how messy it was. I guess Mitch managed to hide it from her until a few days ago." Kyle does a soft laugh after he says this. It makes my heart jump. Or whatever I have inside me. For all I know I'm just a hollow body with no heart or soul.

Where is my soul? It can't be inside me, can it? Or has someone already collected it. There are just too many questions.

"So where are we off to?" Kyle asks, backing out of the driveway.

If we are where I think we are, my old house is about two hours north of here.

171

"Get on the freeway going northbound," I say. I peek at the gas tank. It says we are half-full. "I'll get you some gas money," I say.

"Is this place far?" Kyle glances at me.

I nod. "It's about a two-hour drive. Is that gonna be okay?" All the sudden I'm embarrassed. Why didn't I tell him how far the drive was? He's probably going to think I'm an awful friend. What kind of person asks a stranger to take her far, far away in his brother's car?

A dead one, I guess.

"Road trip," Kyle says.

Music that I've never heard before plays from the radio.

How much earth time did I miss? How much has changed? The music, yes. And the movies.

I glance out the window at the passing cars, and homes. Everything looks the same out there. Even the freeway looks the way I remember it.

"This will be fun," I say. Not sure if it's true or not, but sitting next to Kyle, I no longer have that feeling of worry.

Kyle nods. Then he reaches over and holds my hand. I feel that spark again. It runs through my whole body. It must be butterflies.

My heart jumps again.

35

Me

"**I want to sell** the house," Mom said.

We were on our morning walk. The sun was just creeping up into the sky. It smelled like it had rained the night before, and it made the air cool and damp.

Summer was ending.

"Why would you want to do that?" I asked, even though I already knew the answer. It reminded her too much of Dad. Everywhere we looked was a memory of him.

Hiding in a corner.

In the backyard.

Even the car.

I bet her bedroom still smelled like him. The only thing that didn't remind me of him anymore was the kitchen.

Before, it was always warm, and smelled like something that had just been cooked. Now, it was just a cold, dark kitchen that was almost never used. Except for the few times Mom and I had attempted to cook something special or nice.

"Rosie, we don't need a house that big anymore. I thought I'd have more children when your father and I bought it, but that didn't happen. Now that he's gone, we have all that space that we'll never fill up."

It was true. A month after Dad's death, Mom started to box his stuff up. The only things she left were his clothes in their closet.

Sometimes, when Mom wasn't home, I'd sit on the floor of their closet and look at Dad's clothes. I'm sure it was unhealthy, but it made me feel like he was closer to me.

"But it's our home, Mom. I don't want to move," I said. The sun started to heat things up outside, and I regretted wearing a hat, even though it had been cold when we left the house that morning.

"Wouldn't you like to start over?" Mom said. She looked at me and gave me a sad smile. It made my heart hurt, and I realized she wanted to forget her memories of Dad.

Start a new life. With no more sadness and illness or anything.

I wasn't ready to leave the house I grew up in. I wasn't ready to leave my friends (even if they weren't the best), and I wasn't ready to forget Dad, and all the memories we had.

"I won't move," I said. My voice came out harsh and angry. It had only been a few months. Wasn't there supposed to be more grieving time for us?

"I know this isn't easy for you, Rosie, but we can't live our lives like this. We're holed up in that big, dark, sad home. Don't you want to get out, find some sunshine? Find happiness?"

Mom and I stopped walking when she said this. She sounded like she might cry. I stood there and stared at her. Really looked at her, for the first time in months.

She'd lost a lot of weight. I never really saw her eat anymore. And her hair was losing its color, and so was her skin.

She looked awful.

I wanted to walk over and put my arms around her. But instead I looked away and argued.

"Where do you want us to run away to? Somewhere death won't follow? Somewhere we can start from scratch? Mom, those places don't exist," I said.

Mom gave me a heavy sigh, and then started to walk again.

I waited a minute, and then followed behind her.

"I'm sorry, I'm just being realistic," I said.

Mom stopped walking again, and turned around and looked at me. She had tears in her eyes. "So am I, Rosie. I can't live like this. I can't live with this grief hanging over me like a dark cloud." Then she started crying.

I hadn't seen her cry like that since the funeral.

She reminded me of a child. Standing there with her face in her hands, crying.

These last few months, I hadn't thought about how hard it was for her. All she ever worried about was me.

I was the one who lost her father. Mom was just the wife. She was used to death. Her mother had died when she was young, and after I was born, she had two miscarriages.

She acted like she wasn't that sad. She said she was tough. I always thought she was. But looking at her that day, I realized how sad she really was. How much she had to hide her grief from me. From the world.

It took me a minute, but finally, I walked over and hugged her.

"I'm sorry," I said.

She didn't say anything, though. Just cried while I held her.

I died a week later.

36

Dad

We ride in silence for about forty-five minutes. I watch the other cars pass. Look at the billboards outside the freeway. Advertisements for things I recognize and for things I've never seen before.

Kyle hums along with the radio while he drives. His voice is nice, and it makes the car seem brighter. More relaxed.

"You have a nice voice," I say, after a few songs.

Kyle looks over at me and smiles. He's the type of guy who always seems happy. Someone Mom would have said was a "joy" to be around.

"Thank you. My uncle taught me how to sing. I was embarrassed about it when I was younger. I even sang in church choir. But now I just like humming along to the radio," he says.

I imagine Kyle in a church, belting out songs over a microphone. The thought makes me want to laugh.

"It's nice," I say.

The farther out we drive, the more I start to recognize stuff.

The waterpark where I learned to swim passes by. We went once a year as a family. The big university is coming up in a few miles.

I was supposed to go to school there. Carrie and I talked about it all the time. We always talked about what we were going to do when we graduated. I wanted to stay close to home. She wanted to leave.

"Do you plan on going to college?" I point to a sign telling us how many miles it is to the school.

Kyle shrugs. "Mom wants me to. I don't know. I'm supposed to be promoted to manager in a few months. I might stay here for a few years. Or at least until Penny is a little older," Kyle says. "She's my best friend."

I think of Penny and Kyle. How they laugh together. How much she adores him.

They do seem like best friends.

I wonder what it would be like to have a sibling like that. Always have a friend around.

"You two are cute together," I say. It's the first time I've ever told a boy he was cute. I'm surprised how casually I say it.

Before, I would have died of embarrassment. But I guess since I'm already dead, it doesn't matter.

"Thank you. She really likes you, too, Rosie," Kyle says.

I glance back out my window. And that's when I see it.

The exit that leads to the cemetery where Dad is buried.

It's coming up fast on the left.

"Get off here, here!" I shout, and point to the exit. Kyle swerves and cuts across two lanes, but we manage to make it off the exit.

"Next time, could you give me a little bit of a warning?" Kyle says. He sounds annoyed, but not much.

"Sorry. Just go up two lights and then take a left," I say.

"Where are we going?" Kyle asks.

We're about a half hour from my house.

Mom's house.

Dad insisted he be buried out here, instead of the cemetery by our home. His father was buried out here too.

I hadn't known my granddad, but Dad talked a lot about him.

"If I tell you, will you promise not to think I'm weird?"

Kyle nods. "Of course I won't think you're weird."

That's when I realize I've never seen Dad's grave with anyone other than Mom. Not even Carrie came out here with me.

Sometimes, I would steal Mom's car and drive out here in the middle of the night. And sit by Dad's grave and talk to him.

I knew he wasn't there, but I liked to imagine that he could hear me. From somewhere.

Now I know that wasn't possible. But it still helped with the grieving.

"I'd like to visit my father's grave." When I say it aloud, it feels more real.

Like I'm really here. Like I'm alive, and he's dead.

It's almost as if I never died at all. That somehow my life changed suddenly, and I was dropped in this new world and just picked up where I left off.

But it still doesn't change the fact that Dad's still gone, and I miss him.

"Of course," Kyle says in a quiet voice.

He drives slow to the cemetery. It takes just a few minutes till we get to the gates.

"He's buried on the north side, just go this way." I point and Kyle turns left. We drive for a minute or two more.

It all looks so different, yet so the same.

Kyle parks his car.

I don't get out yet.

I think about the last time I was here. Mom and I hadn't gone together in a long time. So I came out here alone. It was getting cold outside, and I wore one of Dad's coats.

It wasn't even that big on me back then.

I sat and looked at his grave for what felt like hours. I told him about school. Carrie. About how much I wanted a boyfriend, or even just a friend who cared.

I told him how lonely I was, and how much I missed him.

I can't believe how much has changed since now and then.

The trees look thicker and greener. The gates even look like they've aged. With ivy growing all over the fence that surrounds the cemetery.

"You want me to wait in the car?" Kyle asks.

Do I want him to wait in the car? Do I want to do this alone? Can I do this alone?

"No, you can come with me," I say.

Then I get out of the car and head toward my father's grave.

Kyle follows.

37

Black

"I can't do the funeral," I said, lying in bed. Mom stood in my doorway and looked at me. She wore a dark green dress.

Dad's favorite color.

He and I had picked that dress out for her a few years ago for Mother's Day. It brought out the color in her eyes.

Good, I thought, she wasn't going to wear black.

Why did people think black was the appropriate color to wear to these kinds of things? It just made everything seem darker.

Sadder.

Dad was not a dark person, and he rarely wore black.

"Rosie, please," Mom said. She'd been crying all morning. She didn't think I knew, but I could hear her, even through her bedroom door. She tried to hide it, but didn't do that good of a job.

I had been crying too. But not where anyone could see. I stayed hidden under my blankets.

I wanted to run to Dad for comfort, but he was the reason I was crying in the first place. He was never going to comfort me again.

"It's too soon," I said. "I don't want to say good-bye. I'm not ready."

The thought of Dad going into the ground was so final.

It was the end of him.

The end of our family.

Mom walked into my room and sat at the edge of my bed. Even in her grief, she looked nice. Her eyes greener than normal, probably because they were so glossy from tears. The dress was a little baggy on her. She'd lost so much weight in such a little amount of time.

"We have to say good-bye," she said in a quiet voice. "That's how this sort of thing works."

I hated how this sort of thing worked. It shouldn't have to be this way.

And who decided how it was supposed to "work"?

I glanced at my closet. The only dresses I owned were black. I wished so much that I had something green, too. Dad would have liked if I wore green.

"I don't want to wear a stupid black dress," I said. My voice cracked. I could feel tears try to creep up on me. I tried my hardest not to let them fall.

Mom patted me on the hand.

"Who says you have to wear black? Or a dress, for that matter. You can wear whatever you want. Your father didn't care about that kind of stuff," Mom said. She gave me a small smile.

She got up and looked through my closet.

"What about this?" She held out a light blue T-shirt Dad had gotten me years before from a concert he took me to. I remember dreading the concert. Mom said I couldn't go unless Dad took me. I prepared myself for the worst, but it ended up being a lot of fun.

"Really?" I said. Mom nodded.

"Maybe just wear some dark jeans," she said, handing me the shirt.

I got up and took it from Mom. Then I put my arms around her. She smelled nice. Her perfume reminded me of being a little kid. She would wear it when we went to church for special occasions or holidays.

"Thank you," I said.

I was the only one at the cemetery wearing a T-shirt. Carrie had dressed in all black and wore a big black hat.

It reminded me of something you'd see in the movies. Mourning widow attire.

It didn't even surprise me all that much.

Mom and I were both on the program to speak. But I couldn't do it.

Mom cried the whole way through her "speech" about Dad. She talked about the day I was born. And how Dad helped her through her miscarriages. She talked about his cooking, and how if he knew we had cooked funeral potatoes for this, he'd come back to haunt us.

That got a laugh from a few people in the audience.

I didn't find it all that funny, but I smiled anyway.

The whole thing took no longer than an hour. And then it was over.

That was it.

"Come stay at my house," Carrie said as we walked back to our cars. Someone from the morgue drove me and Mom. I hadn't wanted to drive with them, knowing that they saw Dad's dead body. Cleaned it, and all the other stuff they do to the dead. But Mom insisted.

"I can't leave her," I said.

Mom followed behind us, talking to an old woman from our neighborhood. She hadn't wanted to leave before everyone. She wanted to be surrounded by all her and Dad's closest friends.

I was glad about that.

Carrie made a big sigh. "Rosie, she doesn't care. You need me right now." She even wore black lipstick. I had no idea she owned this much black clothing.

For some reason it bothered me seeing her like that. Like this was some sort of fashion show.

"Fine," Carrie said. She knew today was not the day to pester me. Today was not her day, as much as I wished it had been.

"I can't believe you wore that," she said after a second. I stopped and stared at her.

"Are you serious?" I said. She walked ahead a few feet and then turned around.

In that moment I hated her. But worse than that, I envied her. Everything about her.

Her family. Her life.

Everything.

"You have the excuse to wear your favorite color, and go all out, and you wear some dingy T-shirt? I'm surprised, Rosie." She talked to me like this was all a joke. She even let out a small laugh.

I wanted to walk up to her and rip her stupid hat off her head.

I wanted to push her on the grass. I wanted to tear her dress to pieces. I wanted to scream so loud in her face that her eardrums burst.

Instead I just stood there and looked at her. Then I turned around and walked back to Mom.

"Rosie," Carrie said, running up to my side. "Rosie, you know I didn't mean anything by that." Carrie used her fake apology voice, but maybe she was sorry? I know I was.

I turned and looked at her. "I'd like you to leave. Leave me alone." Then I walked over to Mom and grabbed her hand.

Carrie stood there for a minute, but then did as I asked and left.

38

Me

There are yellow roses set on top of Dad's headstone. They look like they are about a day old.

Someone has been here. Recently.

Mom?

Kyle stands next to me while I look at what's written on the grave.

LOVING HUSBAND AND FATHER.

Mom didn't know what to put on there. Never planned on her husband dying. At least not until they were old with grand-children.

My children.

"Do you want me to give you some alone time?" Kyle asks. It's almost a whisper.

I glance up at him. He looks sad. Why did I bring him here?

He probably thinks I'm weird. Has he ever visited a grave? This is the first time he hasn't given me one of those smiles. He just has a faraway look in his eyes.

"Has anyone close to you ever passed away?" I ask.

Kyle looks back down at Dad's headstone. The yellow roses make me sad. Every year for Mom's birthday he got her a dozen of them. She loves yellow. A few years before he died, he even put in a yellow rosebush in the front of our yard.

I wonder if these are roses from my house.

Mom's house.

"My granddad died when I was fourteen. My mom took it pretty hard," Kyle says.

"How did he die?" I ask, not sure if this is an appropriate question to ask. When people asked me about Dad, I was honest, but sometimes it did make me feel worse.

People always want the details.

Lucky for me, Dad's death didn't have many details. Cancer is cancer. The end.

Kyle does a heavy sigh. "He was an alcoholic; he died from liver failure."

"Were you close to him?" A lot of people are close with their grandparents. I never was, but Mom loved her granddad.

"I was close to him the last few years of his life. He took me and Mitch to basketball games and stuff like that. He loved sports. The sad thing is I never really saw him sober a day in his life."

As Kyle continues to tell me about his grandpa, I notice something a few feet from Dad's grave that makes me go cold all over.

Is it what I think it is?

I want to take a closer look, but I don't want Kyle to see me.

How can I tell him to leave me alone while he stands here and spills his guts about his poor alcoholic grandfather?

"You know what I mean?" Kyle says, giving me a strange look.

No, I don't know what he means. What was the last thing he said?

I nod anyway.

"Are you sure you're all right?" Kyle steps closer to me and grabs my hand.

A rush of panic runs through me. I breathe deep through my nose, just stay calm.

Just. Stay. Calm.

"I've just never taken anyone here before," I say. Then I glance behind his shoulder. There's a large statue of an angel just a little ways back.

I always thought she was creepy. That statue. Kind of haunting in a way. I thought of her as the angel of death. Now I know there are no angels of death.

"Maybe you could go over there while I say a prayer at my Dad's grave," I say.

I've never been big on praying, but it seems like the right thing to say.

How else can I get rid of him?

"Sure, if that's what you want. Come and find me when you're done," Kyle says. He doesn't sound offended that I've asked him to leave, but he does look a little bit confused. I walk over and hug him around the neck.

"I'm sorry about your granddad," I say.

"Don't be. I'm glad I got to take you here," Kyle says.

When he's far enough away not to notice me, I walk over to the grave.

ROSIE WOLFE. THE WORLD'S GREATEST DAUGHTER AND BEST FRIEND. MAY SHE REST IN PARADISE.

There's a single yellow rose set down on top of the headstone.

I want to scream.

I want to throw up.

This is what happened to me?

My body is in the ground below my feet.

I touch the top of the headstone. Mom chose a dark gray marble color. Something she knew I would have liked.

Did Carrie help her?

That means they had a funeral.

Did Mom wear the same green dress she wore to Dad's funeral? Did she bury me in my favorite clothes?

Do I even want to know?

I take the yellow rose off the headstone. Mom had to have brought this. She left it here for me.

To remember me.

If I'm here, then who's in the ground?

Or am I just a copy of someone I once was?

39

Home

"**Where to now?**" Kyle says.

We both sit in his car. It's still parked in front of the cemetery. I have my window rolled down. I feel the breeze sneak in every few moments. It smells like fall is around the corner.

I don't know how I feel about this whole trip anymore.

I didn't expect to see my grave.

Or those yellow roses.

"You okay?" Kyle grabs my hand. His skin is soft and every time he touches me my stomach jumps.

Am I okay?

"Just a little emotional I think. Seeing the grave," I say.

Both graves.

Especially mine.

"Any way I can help?" Kyle asks. His tone is soft and sweet. I can't believe someone like him exists, and I only get to be with him at the end of my life.

"Can you take me one last place?" I ask.

I have to know if Mom is still at the house.

I have to see her. Even if she doesn't see me.

"Lead the way," Kyle says.

We get back on the freeway and head to Mom's.

My neighborhood hasn't changed much since I left.

Died.

But it feels different.

Kyle drives slow down the street. We both have our windows open. The warm air that blows into the car smells like a life that was so long ago.

This place isn't mine anymore.

"Rosie? Where should I go now?" Kyle asks.

We're just a few blocks from my house.

A rush of panic runs through me, but I tell myself to relax. I tell myself no one's going to find out you're here.

"Just turn left at the stop sign that's coming up," I say.

Kyle nods.

"So where are we going exactly?"

I guess Kyle has a right to ask, since he's been driving me around all day, but I'm not sure what to tell him.

My house. Well . . . my old house. See, I'm dead, so now it's just my mother's home.

That won't work.

We pull up to the stop sign.

"Would you park for a second?" I ask, trying to buy some time.

Think of something.

"Sure," Kyle says. He gives me that confused look again, but he still does as I ask and parks his car by the curb.

"Can I be honest with you?" I say.

Kyle nods.

"I just want to look at the house I grew up in. Maybe see if I can feel Dad there or something." Is it weird? Does it freak him out? What if Mom's home?

"I'm okay with that, Rosie. I'm fine with driving you wherever you want to go." Kyle uses a light tone when he speaks. The sound of his voice calms my nerves.

It's going to be okay.

Everything's going to be fine.

"How close is the house from here?" Kyle asks. We're still parked on the side of the road.

"Just a few blocks."

Kyle shuts the car and gets out. Then he runs around to my side and opens the door for me.

"What are you doing?"

Kyle grabs my hand and pulls me out of the car.

"Let's walk, Rosie. It's a nice evening and we've been in the car for hours," he says. "We can watch the sunset as we walk."

It'll be dark in a few hours.

I can't imagine what Martha is thinking back at her place.

Is she even home?

Has she called Brandy?

I decide I don't care and get out of the car.

I want to find my mother.

40

Gone

Walking down the streets of my neighborhood, my old neighborhood, makes my heart ache.

The sun is setting, and it makes it that much more nostalgic.

Carrie and I used to sit on her roof and watch the sun set during the summer. It was something we both enjoyed. Sometimes she would sneak beer from her Dad, and we would share a few bottles.

We stopped watching the sky once we both got into high school.

I'm glad that Kyle is next to me, even if he doesn't understand exactly what's going on.

"You lived around here your whole life?" Kyle asks.

My whole life.

My entire life.

I nod.

We walk past yards where I used to play night games with my old elementary school friends. The big tree Carrie fell from and broke her arm when we were just seven. The corner where I had my first and only lemonade stand.

Then we turn the corner and there it is.

Mom's house.

My house.

The shutters outside have been painted light blue, instead of green. The house looks sadder, older, and lonely.

The only thing that really reminds me of home is the rose-bush.

The yellow roses are everywhere.

I walk into the yard, and that's when I see it.

The FOR SALE sign, and below it, a SOLD sign.

Kyle follows close behind me.

"Is this it?" His voice sounds far away. Like he's almost not there. I ignore him and run up the steps to the front door.

Without thinking I start to knock.

"Mom? Mom! Are you in there?" The harder I knock on the door the louder my voice gets. The smell of those yellow roses overwhelms me.

"Rosie, are you all right?" Kyle says. He stands out on the sidewalk and stares at me. Does he look at me like I'm crazy? Is he thinking I'm crazy? Do I even care?

I try to open the door, but it's locked. So I run around back.

The yard has a new chain-link fence around it. Dad would have hated that. I find the gate and go to the back deck.

I peek inside the windows into the kitchen.

It's completely empty.

Even the fridge is gone.

I try the back door, and to my surprise, it's unlocked.

Before I can talk myself out of it, I go in.

The whole house is empty, including my bedroom. My walls have been painted a creamy color. They used to be a pale pink, and my bathroom used to be yellow.

I can't believe Mom's gone.

She's sold the house.

Where did she move? When did she leave? Where is she living?

I go into Mom and Dad's room. The walk-in closet with all of Dad's clothes is empty too. But I sit on the floor in there anyway. Just like I did after Dad died.

I try to breathe in the smell of his cologne. Of the perfume Mom used to wear. I close my eyes and try to imagine that he's here with me. That we're all here together, and all of this has just been a drawn-out bad dream.

"Rosie, are you okay?" I hear Kyle's voice coming up the hall toward where I am.

"I'm back here," I say in a soft voice.

That's when I start to cry.

41

Empty

Why would she want to stay here?

Alone?

Her husband dead, and now her daughter?

Why would Mom want to stay in this empty house alone with no one left?

42

Good-bye

"Rosie, are you all right?" Kyle stands in the doorway of Dad's walk-in closet. I'm still in the corner, trying to pull myself together.

Finish the job.

Get out of here.

But the feeling in the house is keeping me here.

How could she be gone? How could she have left?

"I don't know," I say, staring at the floor. Even though I'm upset doesn't mean I'm not embarrassed. "I'm sorry, I probably seem like a weirdo."

Kyle gives me a smile and then sits down next to me. He puts his arm around my shoulder and pulls me into him.

He smells like happiness.

He smells like someone I want to be around forever.

"I don't think you're weird at all, Rosie. I just don't understand. Why are we here? Where's your mom?" His voice comes out confused, but I can tell he's trying to hide it.

I wish I could tell him where Mom is. I wish I knew.

"This was my dad's closet. The day after he died I sat in here for three hours just breathing in the last of him. For some reason being around his clothes made me feel closer to him," I say.

I've never told anyone that.

Not even Mom knew that I hid in here sometimes. And if she did, she never mentioned it to me.

"I'm sorry about your father," Kyle says. He really does sound sorry.

I look at Kyle. How is he so happy? It's like he's the happiest person on earth. Maybe even in the world. How can that be?

"The truth is I don't know where my mother is. I thought she would be here, but I haven't seen her in a year." Even though it only feels like a few days. "I thought I could come here and she would still live in this house, but it looks like I was wrong," I say.

For some reason I scoot closer to Kyle and rest my head on his shoulder. I breathe him in. I know soon I won't ever be close to him again. I wish I could have had one last moment with Mom like this.

Or Dad.

Where I could just look at them and see that they were real. Alive.

"Do you know where your mom may have gone? Is that why you're living with Martha?" Kyle asks. I know that this must be weird for him.

It's weird for me.

Crazy, even.

I nod. Even though it's not the whole truth. I'm sick of talking about my family. This visit was such a waste.

"Let's go get some food," I say. "There's a diner just a few blocks from here where I used to hang out with my friends. Do you wanna?" Maybe a thick, creamy milkshake will make this sadness at least hide a little bit.

Kyle stands up and then holds out his hand. I take it and we leave Dad's closet.

When we get outside, I take one last look at the house.

The house I grew up in.

The house where my father died.

I'll never come back here. But I'm glad I can say good-bye to it.

I smell one more of the yellow roses and leave.

43

Date

"**It's a double date**," Carrie said. We both sat at Jay's Diner and sipped caramel ciders and hot chocolate.

The place was about to close, so it was just the two of us and the girl working the counter. She walked around and wiped down the tables with a stinky cloth. I could smell it from where I sat a few feet away.

"I've never been on a date," I said. This was just a year or so before Dad died. Boys didn't talk to me unless I was with Carrie. I knew I wasn't the prettiest girl around.

"That's why it's a double. We will be there together. What do you say? Michael says his friend Jake would love to take you out. It's free dinner," Carrie said. She took a sip from her cup.

I did the same thing. Only I burned my tongue on the cider. It was still hot.

"Where is he taking us to dinner?" I asked.

With Dad being a chef, I had a right to be picky about where I ate. Even if it was a free meal. Carrie hated that about me.

"What does that matter, Rosie? It's a date. Not everyone is going to eat gourmet like you," she said. Then she rolled her eyes. Something that she did a lot when I got on her nerves.

We both walked outside to our bikes. It had been raining a lot. The weather was colder than normal, and I didn't like it. The coldest fall we had in years. Just one more year and Carrie and I were going to be able to start driving. I couldn't wait.

"I know that, but I'm just curious. Fine, I'll go on the date. I just don't want it to be awkward."

"All right, well, don't get mad, but Michael wants to come and pick us up now. Late-night mini golf and food after?" Carrie said.

I looked down at my clothes. I looked horrible. Carrie was wearing a full face of makeup and a nice-looking outfit.

I wore a baggy band T-shirt with leggings that had holes in the knees.

"Could I go home and change first and drop off my bike?" I asked.

"You look fine. No one will notice the bleach stain on your pants. And we can come back for the bikes tomorrow," Carrie said, glancing at my legs.

I hadn't even noticed the stain. But now that she had pointed it out, I felt even more nervous.

"Carrie, please," I asked. She ignored me.

I knew there was no point in begging. Carrie had made up her mind. We were going on this date. And I was going to look like a fool.

"Could we just go to a movie then? I don't even know these kids. I don't know if mini golfing will be any fun," I said.

I was starting to panic. I knew I shouldn't have, but I wasn't good at this sort of stuff.

Just breathe, I told myself over and over. But the panic was crawling up my throat.

"Just relax," Carrie said. Then she patted my hand. "It's gonna be fine."

When we got to the mini golf, I regretted ever agreeing to it.

I'd met Michael at school. Carrie had tried to get him to ask her out for weeks. That was one of the only reasons why I had agreed to the date.

The other boy was someone I remembered from years ago. In middle school. He used to tease me with his friends.

I doubted he remembered me, but I was embarrassed anyway.

Carrie didn't even introduce us. Just ran up to Michael and looped her arm around his.

"So much for introductions," Jake said to me.

"Hi, I'm Rosie," I said, holding out my hand. Jake looked at it and laughed.

"This isn't a business meeting, Rosie. You can put your hand away."

I felt my face go red. I wanted to run back to Michael's car and hide in the backseat till all of this was over.

I put my hands in my pockets and followed a few feet behind Carrie, Michael, and Jake. Carrie didn't seem to notice. Every once in a while Jake glanced back at me and laughed.

When we got to the counter to pay, Jake paid for himself and left me there with the cashier.

"It's six dollars," the girl at the mini golf counter said. She didn't look much older than me.

"I didn't bring my purse," I said. I felt my eyes fill with tears.

"I'm just gonna sit over there on that bench until my friends are done," I said.

I saw Carrie a few feet away laughing. Michael had his arms around her waist as she bent over to hit the ball.

Jake stood a few feet from them and looked down at his phone.

"You sure? I could give you my employee discount. It'll only be three bucks," the girl said. She used a tone that I knew well. A tone dripping with pity.

"No, I'm okay," I said. My voice cracked when I said this. Then I stepped out of line and went over to the bench by the door to the building.

The bench was next to an arcade machine that made a loud dinging noise every few minutes.

I waited for about ten minutes before I decided this wasn't me.

I pulled out my phone and dialed Dad's phone number.

"Rosie? What's up?" Dad said. He sounded a little tired on the other end. That's when I realized it was almost eleven.

"Sorry to call so late, Dad. Did I wake you?" I said. He coughed loud, and then cleared his throat.

I woke him up. I could tell.

"No no, not at all. I was just watching TV. What's up? Is everything all right?" Dad said.

When he said this, I felt the tears. The lump in my throat grew bigger.

Before I knew it I was crying.

"Please come and get me, Dad. Please," I said into the phone. The arcade machine made that dinging noise again.

"Where are you?" I could hear him moving around on the other line. Then I heard him get his keys.

He must have fallen asleep on the living room couch

downstairs. Otherwise Mom would be awake too. Asking me why I was crying. Where I was. And all that other stuff moms are required to ask their teenage daughters.

"I'm at the mini golf place. It's about fifteen minutes away. I'm going to start walking," I said. I hadn't even planned it until right then.

I walked out the door and felt a rush of cold air hit me. The first snow of the season decided to start falling at that moment.

How perfect? I thought. *What more could happen?*

"All right, but Rosie, you need to be careful," Dad said.

I walked for about ten minutes before Dad showed up.

When I saw his car, I wanted to cry again. But I didn't.

My hands felt like ice cubes and I could feel a cold coming on when I hopped into Dad's car.

"Where's your coat?" Dad asked. Then he coughed. He had had a cold for what felt like months. Only lately it was getting worse.

"I didn't know I was going to be walking. I left it at home," I said. I wondered if Carrie had even noticed I was gone.

Did that Jake boy even care that I had left? That he was now the third wheel?

I'm sure he didn't even notice. He had his phone to keep him company.

"What happened?" Dad asked.

I shrugged. I was so embarrassed, I couldn't even tell Dad. And he was my best friend.

I felt like a fool.

"How about an omelet. Would that make you feel better?" Every once in a while, Dad and I would stay up and cook a late-night breakfast with each other.

Omelets were my favorite. Those or pumpkin pancakes.

"I still don't want to talk about it," I said. I glanced down at my phone.

No texts or calls from Carrie. *It'll be hours before she realizes I'm gone. If she does at all.*

Will Jake tell her that I ran off? That he didn't pay for me? That he made fun of me when I was trying to be polite?

Probably not.

Dad nodded. And we drove the short ride home in silence. By the time we got into the house it was past eleven.

Dad didn't say anything, just went straight into the kitchen and started cooking.

I changed into dry clothes, and decided to come downstairs and help him cook.

"Want me to make some hot chocolate?" I asked. Dad nodded again.

We cooked together in silence.

When the food was all finished, Dad set us two spots on the table and we sat down. The only light on was the one in the kitchen. It was dark, but outside, the snow made the yard look light.

I took a bite of the food. Everything he cooked tasted better than the last.

"Mmmm, thank you. You're the best," I said, and took another bite. The food was rich and creamy, with thin slices of ham, and spinach and goat cheese on top. I could even taste the butter.

"You ready to talk about it?" Dad asked after a few minutes. The food was half-gone. Dad didn't eat much of his. He'd stopped eating normal meals by then.

"I was supposed to be on a date," I said. I could feel my face go red again. Even though it was just me and Dad, I was humiliated.

"And?" He leaned a little bit in his chair. I think he could tell I was embarrassed.

"And they left me. To pay for myself. And he made fun of me." My voice shook as I spoke. But I kept the tears in. I couldn't cry in front of Dad.

Dad nodded as I spoke and just listened to me talk.

After I told him the whole story, I felt a lot better.

"So what do you think?" I asked. The food was gone and I was feeling warm and cozy in the house. The snow was really starting to come down outside.

"I think that you're an amazing girl. And if you give it time, the right guy will come and sweep you off your feet," he said. "Love finds you when you're not looking for it. Just remember that. When I met your mother, all I wanted was my own restaurant. But she found me, and I never looked back."

He always knew what to say to make me feel better.

I walked over and gave him a big hug around the neck.

"Thank you," I said.

44

Carrie

Jay's Diner is busy, just like I thought it might be. We pull into the parking lot and find a spot right at the front of the building.

The outside of this place looks like a total dump. Just like I remember. It's painted yellow, but all over the building the paint peels off to reveal the ugly brown that's hiding beneath it.

Once I get inside I'm greeted with new booths, a shiny jukebox, and the smell of the best burgers I've ever had.

Even better than Dad's.

"Wow, this place is popular," Kyle says. We stand in the doorway of Jay's, looking for a seat.

I point to a booth a few feet from the jukebox.

"Wanna sit there?" I ask. Kyle grabs my hand and leads the way.

It feels like years since I've been here. But nothing has changed besides the new booths.

"Peanut butter chocolate shake. Doesn't that sound kinda tasty?" I say to Kyle.

He's looking at his menu when I say this.

I suddenly feel self-conscious taking him here. What if he thinks this place is weird, or gross?

Even Dad ate here. So why wouldn't Kyle?

"Peanut butter chocolate? That sounds amazing," Kyle says, looking up from the menu. "Have you decided on what you're going to eat?"

Relief floods over me. I don't know why I'm so nervous. I guess it's just been a long day.

I always got a patty melt when I came here before. A patty melt with a chocolate malt.

"What can I get you two?" I look up from the menu and almost scream.

The waitress stands by our table and stares at me. Our eyes lock and I know she *must* recognize me.

She has to.

No matter what's changed on me, she knows me better than almost anyone in the world.

Carrie.

My best friend.

The last person I saw before I died.

Only she's taller, and her hair is cut short and bleached platinum blond. She wears a dirty apron over her jeans and T-shirt. This is the last place in the world I would imagine her working.

"I think I'll have your peanut butter shake, a grilled cheese, and a cup of soup," Kyle says. He talks like he doesn't notice any tension. And why should he?

Carrie doesn't write down his order, just stares at me.

She looks older because I realize now that she is. It's been a year. She's sixteen now.

I missed my best friend's sixteenth birthday. I missed my own sixteenth birthday too.

"Do I know you?" she asks. Her voice comes out quieter than before.

The rest of the diner is loud. I hear a girl screech a few tables over. I look back down at the menu. It has something sticky on the front. Probably jelly.

"I don't think so," I say.

If Kyle says my name, then I'm screwed. She's going to know it's me.

Unless she already somehow knows it's me.

She had to have gone to my funeral, right? She must have seen me in that box before I was put into the ground.

"Are you sure? What school do you go to?" Carrie steps closer to the table. I feel myself start to sweat. This can't be happening.

I'm going to get caught.

Queen Reaper is never going to let me see Dad.

I'll never see Dad or Mom again.

"I . . . uh . . ." What do I say? I have to think of a lie, and a lie Kyle can't correct me on. "I don't think so." I ignore her question about what school I go to.

"Oh. You look a little like a friend of mine. Remind me of her too. I guess that's impossible," Carrie says. She does a sigh. That's when I look at her again. Her eyes are watery and red. Her hands shake a little bit. I've never seen her like this.

So sad.

She's so different, yet so the same.

"Do you know what you want?" she asks. Her voice sounds

distant, like she doesn't want to be here anymore. She holds up a small pad of paper and a purple pen.

"What happened to your friend?" I don't know why I ask. I should just tell her what I want so we can eat and get out of here. But seeing her makes me miss her. As much as we didn't get along, I realize this is the last time I'll ever see Carrie.

"My best friend. She died at the end of last summer." When she says this, I see a fat tear roll down her face and onto her paper. My eyes start to water.

"That's horrible. What happened?" Kyle asks, handing her his napkin. Carrie grabs it without hesitating. She takes a big breath and wipes her eyes. Then smiles at both of us.

That gorgeous smile. Perfect teeth, just like always.

I wonder if Kyle thinks she's pretty. I think she's gotten even more beautiful. In a sadder way.

"It was a long time ago."

A year ago. It all happened a year ago, even though it feels like it was just a couple days ago.

Does she know where Mom is? Does she know why the house is empty?

"What happened to her family? What happened to her mom?" I blurt out again. Kyle looks at me like I'm being rude.

Because I am being rude.

But I must know. I have to know.

Carrie looks at me again and our eyes lock. She has to see me inside this body. Inside this girl. My eyes haven't changed and neither has my voice, has it?

She pauses for a minute. "Her mom left town. Moved away to stay with her sisters. She told me good-bye. She seemed okay," Carrie says. Now I know she must know.

Must know why I ask.

I think of Mom packing up the house all alone. Packing up my stuff. Packing up the rest of Dad's stuff. Filling her car and driving away.

Never looking back.

Never going back.

"Oh."

Before I can say anything else, Kyle speaks. "I'm really sorry about your friend."

Carrie sighs, but then gives us a small smile. "It's okay. I know she's probably closer to me than I think. Anyway"—she glances at me again—"what can I get you guys?" I start to speak, but she cuts me off.

"How about a patty melt with a chocolate malt?"

Does she really think it's me?

Does she know it's me?

Does it even matter?

"That's exactly what I was thinking," I say.

Carrie nods. "I figured. I'll make sure they grill the onions extra long," she says, and then she smiles again. "My best friend always ordered that here."

Kyle gives her his order again, and she walks back into the kitchen.

"She's a good server," Kyle says. "Knew exactly what you wanted." He smiles at me from across the table.

I listen to everyone around me.

This is where I used to hang out.

My heart hurts thinking about Carrie.

About Mom. But somehow I feel better knowing she's gone. Knowing she's moved on to a better place. Where she's less lonely.

I glance back to where the kitchen is right as Carrie's walking out. She comes straight to the table.

"I know this is weird, but you remind me so much of her. Could I at least hug you?" Carrie says.

I'm shocked when she asks. She never would have asked a stranger that when I was alive.

But I guess I'm not a stranger.

Before I know it tears roll down my face. I wipe them away, but I know Carrie sees them.

"Yes, of course," I say.

I get up and before I know it Carrie is hugging me tight around the neck. I can feel her tears on my shoulder. I breathe her in and she smells just like she always did. Sweet and clean.

My best friend.

"I'm sorry," she says.

And somehow I know that she really is sorry.

Sorry for everything.

45

Done

"**Is there anywhere else** you want to go?" Kyle says.

Seeing the house without Mom being there was disappointing, but seeing Carrie just showed me how real this is.

This is my life now.

I'm dead.

Kyle and I get back to the car. The sun has completely set. We've been gone for hours. Almost the entire day. Martha is probably back at the house right now, freaking out, wondering where I am.

What would have happened if Kyle had seen my headstone? What would have happened if Carrie had said my name? Would they banish me to work at the Office of Death forever?

I'm sick of talking about myself. About my life.

Kyle has been nice to me since the first day we met. Even if

I won't be here much longer, I'd like to listen to him talk.

Just hearing the sound of his voice relaxes me.

"I'm sorry if coming back here was hard for you," Kyle says. He grabs my hand again. I'm actually starting to get used to feeling his touch. The warmth from his soft hands. It's something I thought I would never have.

A boy show affection to me. Even if it is just a small gesture like holding my hand.

"Tell me about your granddad," I say. It's nice having someone with me. Someone like Kyle.

"Well, like I said before, I was young when he died. But he was a good guy, at least toward the end of his life," Kyle says. He stares straight ahead while he drives, like his grandfather is out there, calling to him.

"Do you have any good memories of just you and him?"

The air that comes through the windows is cool. The smell of fall blows past me with the breeze.

The smell that says summer is almost over, and cold is just around the corner.

"He taught me how to ride my bike," Kyle says. Then he laughs. "I had the worst balance of any kid on the street. My mom was worried I was going to have training wheels into adulthood."

As usual, when Kyle smiles, I can't help but smile too. But this time, he looks kind of sad.

"One day, Granddad came over with a screwdriver and told me today was the day the wheels come off."

It reminds me of the day I learned to ride a bike. I was so scared when Dad took the training wheels off, but I learned after just a fall or two.

"I secretly didn't want him to teach me to ride. I wanted my

dad to come home and show me. But he was never around,"
Kyle says. His tone has gone sad. Melancholy.

"Oh, I'm sorry, Kyle. I had no idea," I say. I couldn't imagine
not having my dad around as a kid.

"It's okay. I'm mostly over it now, but sometimes it makes me
mad just thinking about him," Kyle says.

Driving through this neighborhood brings back memories. I
lived here once, and now I'll never be back again. This is the last
time I'll ever see this place.

"So your granddad brought the screwdriver, and then what
happened?" I ask. I try to use a cheerful tone, so Kyle knows I
still want to hear the story.

"He took me to the top of a small hill in our neighborhood,
and said, 'Having a bit of speed will keep your balance. I'll give
you a small push, and then you pedal your little feet off,'" Kyle
says. Then he laughs.

I try to imagine a younger Kyle on a bike. I bet he was a cute
kid. I bet even back then, girls wanted to be around him.

"So what happened after that?" I ask.

"I did what he said, and I pedaled my butt off, and you know
what happened?" Kyle says. He stops the car at a stop sign and
puts it in park.

Why are we stopped?

Kyle turns to look at me. I stare at his eyes. They are like nothing I've ever seen before. So dark, and so shiny.

"You learned to ride your bike?" I ask.

Kyle leans in close and before I know it he's kissing me.

His lips are soft and warm. I don't even have time to panic,
and when he pulls away, I want another kiss from him.

"Wow," I say.

When I was alive, I never kissed a boy before. I never even held a boy's hand.

How come I'm doing all my living after I'm dead?

"What was that for?" I ask. My voice comes out as a whisper. I don't know why, but I'm embarrassed.

What if he stopped kissing me because I'm bad at it?

What do I do if he kisses me again?

"Because I like you. And I knew I would regret it if I didn't do it," Kyle says. Then he clears his throat and starts driving again. "Anyway, I pedaled my bike. I balanced the whole way down, until I crashed into the curb by my neighbor's house. I broke my arm." Kyle laughs. "My mom was so mad. But I never fell off a bike again after that. Even though it was a weird way to teach me how to ride, it worked out."

I laugh. "I liked that memory," I say. Then I lean over and give Kyle a quick kiss on the cheek. I know my face is beet red, but I don't really care all that much. I've finally kissed a boy.

A boy has finally kissed me.

I wish so much that I could run back to Jay's and tell Carrie. Tell her that it's happened, and that he's cool and nice and cute.

"Thank you," I say.

46

Rules

"Where on heaven and earth have you been?" Martha says when I walk in the house.

She has flour all over her shirt and jeans, and her hair looks frizzier than usual.

I'm surprised she's awake, and cooking. But maybe not, since that's what she does when she's stressed.

"Out," I say.

I don't feel like getting into it. I don't even feel like asking Martha why she didn't tell me what year it was, or how close we were to the house I grew up in. I've had too good of a day to fight with her.

I walk past Martha's large body and try to go up the stairs to my room. She grabs me by the arm and pulls me toward her.

"Rosie, I'm responsible for you. So tell me now, or I'm going to write Brandy and tell her all the nonsense you've been up to since you got here. Do you know what will happen if I do that?" Martha says. Her voice comes out harsh and tired. Also a little bit worried. "More souls. Harder souls. You never know."

She looks exhausted.

I almost feel sorry for giving her so much stress these last few days.

Almost.

"Fine." I pull my arm out of her grip and walk into the kitchen. Martha's sanctuary.

Where we always talk.

Today it feels different, though. Darker. Sadder.

"Well?" Martha folds her arms across her chest.

"Well, for starters, you lied to me," I say in a calm voice. I sit down on the barstool by the counter and stare at her.

Thinking about it makes me want to cringe. But I don't want to lose this good feeling I have. The feeling Kyle left me with. I want to hold on to it forever.

"Lied to you how?" Martha asks.

"I went with Kyle to visit my father's grave. You failed to mention how close I was to where I grew up, and you lied. You didn't tell me I'd lost a whole year while I was up there," I say.

Why didn't she just tell me?

Why does all of this have to be such a huge secret?

"Where's my mother?" I ask.

Martha does a heavy sigh, then opens the fridge and pulls out a dark-looking beer. I've never seen her drink before. Then she goes to the cabinet above the sink and gets out her pack of smokes, and lights one up.

She sits on the chair next to me.

"I didn't lie, Rosie. You never asked, so I never told you. Time is different for the living and the dead." She lights up a smoke and inhales it.

"I don't know where your mother is, and that's the truth. They don't give me that kind of info. What they tell me is limited. But listen to me," Martha says while opening the beer. She pours it into a tall glass. It looks like the kind of beer Dad would drink after a long day. He wasn't much of a drinker, but every once in a while, he would have a beer and sit in front of the TV and relax.

At least before he got sick.

"Listen close. Rosie, you're going to regret spending all this time with Kyle. You're going to regret getting to know him. You aren't supposed to come down here and make friends, you're supposed to do your job," Martha says. Then she takes a sip of beer.

"I've seen this before. And when it's time to leave, you're going to have a hard time with it. You can't take him with you, Rosie. He stays here. And that's that," Martha says.

I can smell the beer. It's totally the kind Dad drank.

I reach over and grab the glass and take a sip.

It's rich and creamy, with a bitter aftertaste.

I hate it. But I want more.

"Rosie, stop." Martha takes the beer from me. "Focus on what I'm telling you, please."

I am listening to her. I just don't like what she has to say.

"I know I can't take him with me, but I don't think you know how it feels. Being dead. Not feeling real. He makes me feel alive again," I say. I know it's corny, but it's true.

Being with him today I felt more normal than I ever have my whole life.

Alive or dead.

It was like I was a regular girl, with a regular boy, who wanted to be with me. To spend time with *me*.

"Boys never liked me before. This is the first time someone like him has showed me even a bit of attention. It makes me feel good, especially when I'm feeling so sad."

I sound pathetic and dramatic when I say this, but I don't really care.

Martha looks at me like she feels sorry for me. Then she reaches over and gives my hand a squeeze.

"I know what you're feeling, Rosie. But I'm here to help you, and I don't want you to do something you're going to regret. I can't let you break the rules. Otherwise, we could both get into trouble. Do you understand?" Martha talks to me like I'm a child. And I don't blame her.

She's right.

I have been breaking the rules.

I can't be the only Reaper who ever has?

I'm sure all of us do. At least once or twice on our visit back down here.

"I just want to get my last soul and finish this," I say. Even though I want to get out of here, I know I'm going to miss Kyle. Martha is right about that. He won't be able to come with me, but at least I'll have the memory of him.

And will I meet him when he dies?

Will he come to the same paradise as me?

I guess I won't know until I get back Upstairs.

"I'm going to go to bed," I say. I lean over and give Martha a hug.

"I'll be down here if you need me. The last soul will come tomorrow. So get your rest."

I walk upstairs and fall onto my bed.

I sleep like a baby.

47

Envelope

"Rosie. Rosie!"

I open my eyes and see Martha standing above me. She holds a purple envelope and waves it in front of my face.

"It came. It's the last soul," she says.

She sounds excited. I bet she's glad to get rid of me and all the trouble I've caused her.

"Get up and let's eat some breakfast. I'll make you French toast, to celebrate," Martha says.

I sit up and stare at her.

"Why are you so happy?" I ask.

Martha tosses me the envelope and then points to it. "Once you collect that soul, it's my weekend. I can leave this house for four days. I'm going to Vegas," she says. Then she does a small dance and walks out of my room, with what you would call a skip in her step.

I change out of my pj's and wash up. Then go downstairs to where Martha is cooking homemade stuffed French toast.

"Smells great," I say.

"Thanks. It's your father's recipe, but with a twist," Martha says, holding up a bottle of rum. She pours a few tablespoonfuls into the heavy cream, and then whips it up.

"Drunken stuffed French toast," I say. Martha nods.

"Have you opened it yet? Should we bet it's an old woman?" Martha says while whipping the cream.

"I don't really care, I just want to get it over with. This is the worst part," I say.

Collecting the souls always makes me sick and depressed. But I'll be glad when it's over. Even though it means I won't ever see Kyle again.

My heart jumps at the thought of last night.

Cuddling, kissing, the way he smelled while I was next to him. Will I ever feel that?

Do people get married in paradise? Or was this life their one chance at love?

"These will cheer you up," Martha says, handing me a plate of the French toast. There's a dollop of whipped cream on each piece. I can smell the rum and cinnamon; it makes my mouth water.

"Thank you," I say. They taste better than Dad's. I don't know how she does it, but she outdoes him every time.

"I learned from the best," Martha says. Then she sticks her finger in the whipped topping and licks it off. "That's got a nice little kick to it."

She makes herself a plate of food and sits next to me at the counter.

"Stop thinking about that boy," she says.

Of course she knows that's who's on my mind. How could he not be?

"I can't help it," I say. I take another bite of the food.

I hope I can eat like this when I go Upstairs. If not, Dad is going to have a fit. Do they let him cook?

"Will I ever see him again? I mean, after I collect that last soul?" I ask. I know that Martha doesn't have all the answers, but all I can do is ask.

I take another bite. This is my favorite meal I've had yet.

"When he dies, and if you two choose to see each other. But Rosie, this isn't the end. There are other fish in the sea, even if that sea isn't on earth," Martha says. "Even if that sea is full of dead fish." She laughs at her own joke and then takes a bite of the French toast.

"People fall in love after they move to paradise?" I ask.

"Of course they do. Paradise *is* love. What's paradise without love? Oh, Rosie, you have a lot to learn."

For some reason I feel relieved. It's not like I plan on marrying Kyle or anything. But at least I won't have to leave him behind forever.

At least he will know, one day, that he has been the nicest boy I've ever met.

"Now open that envelope. Let's get this job over with," Martha says.

I take the envelope and walk into the living room and sit on the couch. Martha follows with her plate of food.

"Will you open it for me? I'm too nervous," I say, handing Martha the lavender-colored envelope.

"I guess." She sets her plate down on the coffee table and takes the letter from me.

She doesn't waste any time, and rips the top off it and pulls out the paper.

"Congratulations," Martha reads aloud. *"You have made it to your last soul. You're just a few hours away from returning to your new home in paradise where your friends and family are waiting. Your instructor,* that's me," Martha says, pointing to herself, *"will walk you through the last steps. Attached is the info of your last soul."*

She flips the page.

When Martha starts reading, her face drops. It's lost almost all its color.

"What's wrong?" I ask.

What could that sheet of paper say? Who could it be?

Martha ignores me and walks into the kitchen with the paper in hand.

"Martha, tell me. What's wrong? Who's written on that sheet of paper?" But I can tell by the look on her face it must be Kyle.

I have to take Kyle, don't I? I knew it. The second I touched his hand, I knew I was going to have to collect his soul.

Cause him to die.

"It's Kyle, isn't it," I say. I jump up and run into the kitchen. "I can't believe it. I can't take Kyle. Please," I say.

Martha still holds the paper. Tears spill out of her eyes.

"It's not Kyle, Rosie," she says.

"Then who is it?"

48

Tonight

"**Why don't you stay** with me tonight?" Mom said. She sat on my bed while I looked through my closet.

Carrie and I were going to opening night of *The Black Bird,* and Carrie had told me that a lot of cute guys were going to be at the after-party her friend was having.

"I can't, Mom. I promised her I would go. Plus, I need to get out of the house."

Mom looked so tired, like she didn't really care if I went or stayed. Just as long as she could be in bed early.

"You don't have to wait up for me either, I probably won't be back till after midnight," I said.

Mom shrugged. "I was hoping we could spend the weekend together. I feel like I haven't seen you in days."

She was right about that. I had been avoiding the house like the plague those last few weeks. I don't know if it was the fact that we had just come up on the one-year anniversary of Dad's death, or if it was something completely different. All I knew was I didn't like the feeling in the air.

"Maybe we could go on a hike and picnic or something tomorrow," I said.

Mom and I had been doing more and more outdoor activities with each other. Our morning walks had turned into hikes up the canyon.

"You sure you wanna spend your Saturday with me?" Mom asked, smiling. She got off my bed and looked through my closet with me.

Black.

Black.

Black.

"Maybe I'll just wear the jean skirt and this button-up," I said, more to myself than anything else. The shirt was a gray button-up. I'd never worn the jean skirt, but it had been in my closet for at least two summers.

"Will it be too cold? It's getting chilly in the evenings." Mom eyeballed the skirt. "Plus it's supposed to rain," she said.

"I'll be fine."

I ran into the bathroom and changed my clothes. When I showed Mom, she grinned.

"Beautiful. I can't believe how grown-up you look." She touched the bottom of my skirt. It was short. But I kinda liked it.

"Thanks, Mom," I said. Then I laughed. "Maybe I'll get a date." I used a sarcastic tone.

We both knew that was never going to happen.

No one had ever asked me out.

I was fifteen years old, and not a single boy had ever called my house to talk to me.

But maybe tonight could be different? Maybe I could meet someone?

"Don't use that tone," Mom said. "You never know. Maybe tonight you'll meet the boy of your dreams."

I hadn't even really thought about what the boy of my dreams would look like.

"You're so corny," I said.

"Just have confidence, Rosie. You deserve someone nice to take you out every once in a while."

Mom grabbed the brush off my desk and ran it through my hair.

It felt nice. It reminded me of when I was a little girl. She would French braid my hair for fancy dinners, or sometimes put ribbons in my hair.

I loved it.

"Wear your hair down tonight. It's getting so long," Mom said. Her tone sounded kind of sad when she said this. I turned to look at her and she was crying.

"Mom, what's wrong?" I put my arms around her. She hardly ever cried, so when she did, it worried me.

"I love you so much, and I just wish your father could see how much you've grown this last year."

When she said this, a lump formed in my throat.

The tears were trying to fight their way out of me, but I wasn't going to let it happen today. I wasn't going to cry.

Tonight was going to be a good night.

Tonight, my life was going to change, because I was going to meet someone. I just knew it.

"He can see me. From somewhere, I'm sure he can see me," I said.

Mom nodded when I said this. Then she wiped the tears from her eyes and composed herself as if nothing had ever happened.

"You're right, Rosie. He's watching over us," she said. "Remember that when you plan to kiss a boy tonight."

"Gross, Mom," I said. Then laughed.

She walked me downstairs to the front door. For some reason that feeling was still in the house. I couldn't tell if it was a bad or good feeling. But whatever it was, it was stronger than ever.

"Are you sure you don't want a ride?" Mom asked.

I shook my head. "It's only a few blocks," I said.

Mom put her arms around me and gave me one last hug. "I love you, Rosie girl. Be careful, and call me when you get to the theater."

The last hug she ever gave me.

"I love you, too," I said.

Then I walked out the front door. Right to my own death.

49

Brandy

"Tell me this is a joke," I say to Martha.

Penny Morales.

They want me to take Penny Morales's soul.

It's even worse than taking Kyle.

"It's not a joke," Martha says. She paces around the living room while I look at the paper. "I just don't know why they would want to take that sweet little girl's soul, and in such an awful way," Martha says.

I haven't once considered that the people who die around her are her neighbors, even her friends.

Taking Penny won't just affect her family. It'll affect everyone who has ever met her.

Including me.

"I have to call Brandy," I say. I've tried to stay calm. I've watched my breathing. But I can feel the panic rising in my throat.

I run upstairs and grab my cell phone.

It rings before I can even dial the number.

It has to be her. Brandy.

"Yes?" I say. My voice comes out rough and scratchy. Like maybe I'd had a cold for weeks.

"Rosie, hi. It's Brandy. Did you get the last name? I'm preparing everything up here for your return. How long do you think it'll take you to collect that soul?" Brandy sounds cheerful today. "I know the cause of death is kind of tricky, so make sure you do it soon. You probably only have an hour or two. What time is it there anyway?" Brandy says.

I pause before I respond.

How can she be so relaxed? Knowing that a little girl will die. An innocent little girl, who never did anything to anyone except be alive and happy.

"I don't know, like nine thirty or something," I say. Brandy's voice is like a drill in my ears. A happy, chipper drill. If I had heard from her last night, I would probably be happy. But not now.

Not anymore.

"Brandy," I say while she chats on about I don't know what. It's almost as if she can't hear me.

"Brandy!" I shout into the phone.

"What?" she says. Her tone sharpens a bit, but not too much.

"I need you to listen to me. Are you listening?" I walk back downstairs to where Martha is. She's started cooking something. As usual.

"Yes, yes, what is it, Rosie?" I imagine Brandy at her desk. Examining her nails. Drinking her cup of coffee. Ruining other people's lives . . . or I guess, afterlives.

Even though I know none of this is her fault, I'm still so upset I could pull her hair out.

"I can't get that last soul. I can't do it," I say. My voice starts to crack. I can't cry. Not right now. Not on the phone.

"Oh, this again. What's the problem now, Rosie? You said that about Cody Bingham and you got him just fine. You're just overstressing because it's the last soul. You Reapers always do this," Brandy says. She sounds annoyed with me.

But she's wrong.

This isn't the same. It's not the same at all.

"Have you even read who the soul is, Brandy? Have you read how she dies? I can't be responsible for that," I say.

I hear Brandy moving around what sounds like papers. "Ahh, here it is. Your final name. Penny Morales, age four. I guess I can see why that's hard. But from the looks of your file, you've been sent this soul as punishment," Brandy says. "You touched her brother."

Just hearing it read out loud makes me want to scream. I wish there was a way for me to hide Penny. To protect her from what's coming.

What I've brought her.

To protect her from me.

"You know the rules, Rosie," Brandy says. It's true, I do. But I don't care.

"So you're killing this little girl because I broke a couple rules?" I shout in the phone.

What kind of job is this?

These people are heartless. They have no souls.

"Brandy, I can't. She lives across the street from Martha. I can't take the soul of someone I know," I say.

Sweet little Penny. Kyle's best friend.

I haven't even thought about Kyle.

What will he do if she dies? He won't be able to handle it. Not after his dad left him. They're so close.

"Rosie, that's not my problem. She's going to die either way. She's just been assigned to you. This is what happens. You're lucky that Death is letting you off with such a small punishment." Brandy sounds annoyed and tired. Like this conversation shouldn't even be happening.

And it shouldn't.

"I'll get everything worked out up here. Just take the soul as soon as possible so you can come back," Brandy says. Then hangs up the phone.

"I never agreed to this!" I shout, and then I throw the phone across the room.

"Did you have any idea this was going to happen, Martha?" I say.

She stirs a pot of boiling water. It smells like soup. It's not even lunchtime and she's already preparing dinner.

"How could I have known, Rosie? I wouldn't have let you go near that house if I had known they were going to take her," Martha says. Her voice cracks and I can tell she's trying not to cry again.

"I can't do it. How am I supposed to do it? She's too sweet. She's such a pure soul," I say.

Martha nods like she knows. Because she does know. She's lived across the street from her since she was born.

"You still have to take her, Rosie. You do know that, don't you?" Martha says.

If I don't, I'll never see Dad again. At least not for a very long time. But if I do, I'll ruin Kyle's whole family's lives.

But if I don't take her, someone else will.

"I know that," I say. And it's true. But it doesn't mean I like it. I didn't agree to this. You shouldn't be punished because you die.

"You're losing time, Rosie. I suggest you go over there and do it now. It takes a few hours for the souls to go, you better go now," Martha says. Then she turns around and throws her big arms around me.

That's when Martha loses it.

She cries louder than anyone I've ever met. And I cry right along with her.

50

Penny

Kyle's mom answers the door when I knock.

"Rosie, how are you?" she says, letting me inside. The house is quiet except for the TV that plays in the living room.

"I'm all right, how are you doing?" I ask, trying to sound cheerful.

I can hear Penny in the living room, giggling at the TV. Sometimes talking to the TV. Hearing her laugh makes me want to turn around and run home.

But I can't.

I have to do this.

I get to see Dad soon.

"I'm good, but Kyle and Mitch are at work until four. Is that why you're here?" Carolina asks.

Good. I'm glad I won't have to see Kyle.

Let things end with how they were last night.

It almost feels like it never happened. The kisses. The sweet things he said to me.

It was like a dream. A dream that ruined everything.

If I hadn't been so selfish, I wouldn't have to be here right now. Ruining everything for this family.

"Oh, okay. Well, can I say hi to Penny?" I ask.

Carolina nods. "Sure! She's just in the living room watching TV." I follow her into the living room, where Penny sits on the couch. She wears her swimsuit and flip-flops. Her dark hair has been braided into pigtails as usual.

"Penny. You have a guest." Penny turns around and sees me and grins.

"Rosie!" She jumps off the couch and puts her little arms around my legs in a hug.

"I'll let you chat," Carolina says, and leaves the room.

I sit on the floor and pat the spot next to me.

Penny plops down next to me on the light pink carpet and starts chatting before I can get a word in.

"Are you here to swim with me? Mom found her swimsuit, I bet it'll fit you. We can have a splashing war. Me and Mom did yesterday. It was fun," she says.

I shake my head.

"No, I'm getting ready to leave. I just wanted to say bye to you. And thank you for being such a good friend to me," I say.

Penny's eyes are so shiny, and she has that same contagious smile as Kyle. Only I'm not smiling now.

I use everything I have not to scream at the top of my lungs.

"Where are you going?" Penny sounds sad and confused.

"I've got to go home. I'm going to see my father, but you and me, we will meet again. Someday," I say. I feel the tears start to fight their way out, and this time I let it happen. I try to hide them but Penny notices.

"What's wrong?" she asks.

"I'm just going to miss you is all," I say.

"You'll visit again soon, right? Then we can go swimming," Penny says.

I nod.

Penny leans over and gives me a big hug around the neck. I reach over and touch her shoulder.

Instantly I feel her soul. But instead of it being cold, it's warm and light. It's like I've just woken from a great dream.

Light like a summer rain on a hot day.

"I'll miss you," she says. Then she leans over and kisses me on the cheek.

She doesn't sound sad, just hopeful. Like someday she really will see me again.

"Look for me when you get older," I say.

Penny lets go of me, and I stand up and walk toward the door. The warm feeling has left, and now I just feel sad and alone.

I want to run back to her and take her with me.

I hope there will be someone waiting for her on the other side. I hope she's too young to do the reaping, and she can go to paradise with no worries.

"Bye, Rosie," Penny says.

I run out the front door before I can say anything else.

51

Good-bye

"This isn't the end. You'll see me again," Dad said on his last night. Mom and I were next to him at the hospital. There were so many tubes, and beepers, and needles that I wanted to run away.

This wasn't how I wanted to remember Dad.

Attached to a machine.

Mom held on to his hand. His skin was gray. Like there wasn't much left of him.

I hated when he talked about death, but I knew this was the end. Now was the time to say my good-byes to him, because I didn't know how many hours he had left.

How much longer he would be awake.

"How do you know?" I asked. I'd been crying all day. I couldn't stand the thought of it. That he was leaving me.

Forever.

I was never going to see him again.

"Because I know," he said.

Mom looked like she'd aged about ten years those last few days. I could tell she had gotten less sleep than me.

"Josh, you have to keep fighting, please don't give up," Mom said.

Dad had outlived what the doctors said. They gave him six months, and he'd made it past nine. Around month ten is when things started getting really bad.

"He is fighting," I said. Dad's eyes were closed, but he still spoke in a calm and soothing voice.

"When I leave, I want you to start cooking, Rosie. Your mother is going to need all the help she can get. She's a worse cook than you," he said.

Mom and I laughed at that, even though we were both crying our eyes out by then.

"I will, Dad. I love you." I leaned up and kissed his face. His skin was cold and dry.

"I love you too, Rosie girl," Dad said.

Then he opened his eyes and turned to Mom.

"You're the love of my life. Don't ever forget that," he said.

Mom leaned up and kissed him softly on the mouth. "I love you," she whispered.

We listened to him breathe for hours and hours.

He didn't say anything else after that.

But he died the next night.

I was always grateful that we got to say our good-byes.

52

Heart

Martha makes me a hot cup of cider and sends me upstairs to rest before I make the trip home.

The warm feeling I got from Penny has turned sick and cold, just like the other souls. It's only been an hour, but I bet she's almost gone.

I can tell by the way I feel on the inside.

The cider doesn't make me feel much better, but at least it's something.

I can't help but think about her.

The hug and kiss she gave me, and how sweet she was when I met her.

How much Kyle loves her.

The thoughts break my heart.

I realize now that I do have a heart. And it's broken for Kyle and his family.

Martha warned me. She warned me over and over again that I would regret getting close to them. But I couldn't help it.

I'm about done packing my things when I hear the doorbell ring.

Is it someone coming to get me? To take me back Upstairs to where Dad is?

"Rosie," Martha calls.

I grab my bags and head downstairs. I'm not sure how I'll get back, but right now, I don't care.

When I get to the bottom of the stairs, my jaw drops.

It's Kyle.

He seems happy enough. Like nothing has happened.

"Rosie, you're here."

He runs over to me and puts his arms around my neck. "Penny told me you were leaving. I had to come and say bye," he says.

She's still alive.

Or at least she was when Kyle walked over here.

Maybe they don't want her? Maybe Death changed her mind and decided to take someone else.

A spark of hope hits me, but only for a second. Because I know that can't be true.

But I wish so much that it were.

"Yeah, I'm about to leave," I say. Talking to him makes me feel worse than I ever have. I want to spill my guts right now and tell him what's going to happen. I feel sick, sick with guilt. And regret.

But soon I will be gone, and soon so will she.

Penny.

All because I came into Kyle's life. All because I was selfish. Because I refused to follow the rules.

His best friend will be dead because of me.

"I was hoping you'd come over for just a second to tell every-one else good-bye. My mom was bummed when Penny told her you were leaving," Kyle says.

Go back over there?

How could I possibly do that?

"I don't know if that's a good idea," I say. But the look on Kyle's face tells me I need to. Or maybe I have to.

"Martha is waiting." I point toward the kitchen. I can hear her cooking in there.

I glance back at Kyle. He looks sad. Disappointed.

Because I'm leaving. I know that without having to ask.

"Could you, please? Just for a few minutes?" he says.

I hesitate but then nod.

What more could I do to this family?

I follow Kyle outside and we head to his house.

It's so hot, but I feel cold on the inside. Like I know something bad is going to happen.

Because something bad is going to happen.

Kyle looks at me and smiles, but I don't smile back.

The sun shines down hard on us and makes the colors in his hair bold and vibrant.

I hear something in the distance that sounds like a scream. Or maybe a cry.

We get closer to his house and that's when I see his mom. She kneels next to the kiddie pool, and in her arms she holds Penny's body.

"Oh my God," Kyle shouts.

We both run over to where his mom is on the grass.

Penny in her swimsuit, her hair soaking wet. When I look at her, I know she's gone.

Her lips are blue, and the color is drained from her face.

I've never seen a child's dead body before. So small and frail. Almost like a doll.

Seeing Penny like this now makes me want to screech. Not with terror, but with grief.

She's so little. So innocent.

"Help. Kyle, Mitch! Help. She's not breathing," Carolina says. I've heard that same tone so many times. From my mom's own voice. When Dad was dying. So panicked and scared.

It's almost like watching a movie. Like standing outside of a scene that you shouldn't see.

"No, no!" Kyle grabs Penny's body from her. He lays her on the grass and tries to bring her back.

He tries to save her.

"Penny. No. Please, no. Wake up," he says. Pulls her up onto his lap and cries.

His cry is like nothing I've ever heard before.

His mom is crying now too.

"Help. Someone help," she keeps screaming. I'm not even sure who she's calling to. Another neighbor from across the street runs over to where they are. "Someone call nine-one-one!" they shout.

I see a family head toward us. Another one of Kyle's neighbors. Probably other people who know and love Penny.

What should I do? Is there something I can do? More than what I've already done? I feel frozen and hollow.

I step closer to Kyle.

Could I save her? Is there a way to undo what I've done? To bring her back?

How do people come back from the dead? Do people come back from the dead?

A breeze rolls in and I get goose bumps. There are so many of Kyle's neighbors around me. All of them trying to help.

Why can't I help?

There must be a way to undo this.

"Penny. You can't die," I say out loud. "You're not supposed to die, this wasn't supposed to happen." Now I'm crying too.

"Please don't die," I say, quieter this time. "Please don't die."

The shouts surround me. Kyle. Carolina. Now the neighbors. Does Kyle hear me? Does Penny?

But maybe Death can.

Why would she want me to take someone like Penny? Why?

Mitch, Kyle's older brother, shoves me out of the way.

"Penny!" he says.

This family is real. This family loves one another. And I've torn them apart. Like my family was when Dad died.

"Please don't die," I say again.

And then I turn and run.

I run as fast as I can.

Penny.

Kyle.

Dad.

Me.

Death doesn't care who it takes. Doesn't care if you're a dad, a little girl, a teenager. Death doesn't care who you are or what you've done. Doesn't care how much you mean to someone else.

I hear an ambulance in the distance. Who called them? Mitch? His mother?

I keep running.

I just have to get away from their shouts. Their cries. Their pain. The same pain that I've felt a million times. That my family felt a million times.

242

All because of me.

All because of Death.

All because of Life.

When I get to Martha's, I see the ambulance drive past and I know that even though it doesn't end here for Kyle, my time is done.

Martha stands next to me and cries. She grabs me tight around the arm. "The guilt will go away, I promise," she says through her tears.

Penny.

I hope so much that they don't make little babies like her reap souls. She's so sweet and innocent. It wouldn't be fair. She's not even had a chance to live.

But I guess neither did I.

We walk back into the house and I feel like I will never recover.

Like no matter what happens after this, after I move on, that I'll never feel better.

We both sit in her living room on one of the couches. The house smells just like it did that first morning I was here. Just a few days ago, my only worry was getting back Upstairs. I had no idea what was going to happen.

It feels like that was so long ago, even though it's only been a couple days.

"It smells nice," I say. I don't cry anymore.

The tears are gone. They've all dried up.

I breathe in the smell of cinnamon rolls and think of the whole reason I'm here.

The whole reason I did this.

Dad.

Will it be worth all the pain I caused? The pain I've gone through?

"I thought I would make you a farewell snack. Even though you've been a huge pain in my ass, I'll miss you," Martha says. She's still crying and before I know it she has her arms around me again.

So much crying today.

Her arms are heavy around my shoulders, but there's something comforting about her hug. It gives me hope that this *is* all worth it.

53

Now

I open my eyes to see the ceiling of a yellow room. I look around and notice I'm in a bed. The softest bed in the world. The blankets remind me of being a baby and something about them seems familiar.

I look around, and everything is so bright I can't see the detail.

The windows are open and the breeze that comes through is the perfect temperature. Smells like spring but looks like summer.

I glance back down at the blanket. It's the one Mom made me when I was a baby. Soft and warm. I put it to my nose and inhale.

It smells just like her.

Mom. I miss her so much. But my heart doesn't ache anymore, because something tells me she's okay. That I'll see her again someday.

I roll out of bed and look around the room. It's filled with memories of my life. I don't know how, but I can picture my whole life in this bedroom. I see memories of Mom holding me. Images of Dad cooking with Mom in the kitchen. Of times with me and Carrie laughing in her bedroom. Of Kyle kissing me that day in the car.

Of Penny hugging me good-bye.

All the memories play out in my head. On the walls of this room. Everywhere.

How?

It must be a dream.

A dream I don't ever want to wake up from.

I walk to the door and open it.

Now the smell of Martha's cinnamon rolls fill my room. I forgot that she was baking them.

Of course Martha is in my dreams. Why wouldn't she be?

Out in the hallway the brightness of everything almost hurts my eyes. I go to the edge of the stairs. The smell gets stronger. Sweet and spicy. My mouth waters.

I go down the stairs into the kitchen. It's even brighter in there.

But my eyes can see clearly and the feeling of the air around me makes my heart sing.

I've never felt so happy, and I don't know why.

Then I see him.

Standing there, smiling.

I almost think my eyes are playing a trick on me. I blink.

Once.

Twice.

Three times.

He doesn't leave.

He stands there and stares at me, smiling.

"Rosie, I've been waiting for you," he says. He opens his arms and I run to him.

It's really him.

He's alive.

He's real.

"Dad."